WRITERS ANARCHY IV
Horror

Published by Fiction Writers Group

Other Books by Fiction Writers Group

Writers' Anarchy I

Writers' Anarchy II: The End of the World as We Wrote It

Writers' Anarchy III: Heroes & Villains

Flash It!

Anything Goes, Volume I

Anything Goes, Volume II

Dedication

This short story collection is dedicated to the members of Fiction Writers Group, without whom our anthologies would not be possible. To all of the members who volunteer their time, experience, and skill for the many, this is for you.

Copyright Notice

Published by Fiction Writers Group

Writers' Anarchy IV: Horror

First Edition, October 2015

Edited by Alex Hurst

Book design copyright © 2015 Linda Laforge
LindaLaforge.com

Cover design copyright © 2015 Country Mouse Designs
countrymousedesigns.com

Individual stories and characters © 2015 by their respective authors.

All stories used with permission of their respective authors granting non-exclusive rights to publication and distribution.

All rights reserved.

No part of this book may be reproduced, scanned or distributed to any printed or electronic form without the express written permission of the authors. Please do not participate in or encourage piracy of copyrighted materials in violation of the authors' rights.

Purchase only authorized eBook or print editions.

These are works of fiction. Names, characters, locations and occurrences are the product of the authors' imagination or are used fictitiously, and resemblance to any actual persons, living or dead, events, locations or business establishments is entirely coincidental.

ISBN-13: 978-1519448248

writersanarchy.com

Table of Contents

The Collector *by Terri Zeller Wallace*
1

He Walks in My Black *by Paul Draper*
13

Granny Mabel *by Danielle C Allen*
20

Sabine Baring-Gould and the Werewolf *by Roy C. Booth*
26

Walk A Mile *by Paul Mannering*
34

Jennah *by John Mc Caffrey*
40

The Shadows Draw Long *by Joseph Y. Roberts*
52

The Mask *by Jim Tritten*
64

Redemption Dog *by HMC*
78

Quietly, Ross *y Kerry E.B. Black*
84

All He Loved *by Kelly Haas Shackelford*
93

Clandestine *by T.D. Harvey*
99

A Note *by Raitt Black*
112

Arachnight *by Angela J. Maher*
128

Absent Friends *by John Lau*
141

Nasty Little Nightmare *by V. Jáuregui*
160

The Collector

by Terri Zeller Wallace

Granny Enid didn't want to take me in at first. The social worker really had to work at her to get her to agree to it. I thought it was me—maybe she thought I was bad luck or jinxed or something, seein' how Mama died and all. But it wasn't me; it was just one of those secrets that I didn't know about until much later. Granny was right, though. It would've been better if I'd stayed away.

When I first arrived at Granny Enid's, Crankston's Landing was finishin' off the driest summer on record. The white sedan that the social worker drove was covered in a thick red film from the Oklahoma dirt, which seemed to cover everything that year. A white cat sat on the rail of the porch, and when it stretched out I could see the red-stained fur matted on its underbelly. No matter how much that cat licked and cleaned, the stain never came off.

No one answered the door when I knocked. I looked back at the social worker, her dark hair clipped back with a fake pearl barrette, sittin' in her air-conditioned car, and she motioned for me to try around back. I clutched the plastic grocery bag that held my spare socks and underwear in my sweaty palm, and I followed the path to a gate that was half rotten. It might've been painted white once; now it just shared the same reddish tint as the cat. The hinges squeaked when I shoved the gate open enough to slip through it.

I wish I could say that on the other side of the fence it was a lush green paradise, but it wasn't. Everything in that backyard was dead—the yellowed grass, the withered honeysuckle, the pile of rotting kitchen scraps, and the remains of a tiny kitten left near the trash cans. The smell made me throw up the apple cinnamon waffles that I had eaten at the Waffle Barn just off the interstate. The social worker had bought them for me, and she even let me have extra syrup.

When I cleared every last crumb off my plate, she had pushed her plate across the table. "Eat it," she said. "Go on—I'm full." So I did. But now it was spewed all over the ground.

"Junie?" a voice called from the back porch, and I turned to see a hunched figure limping towards me. "That you, Junie Rae?"

"Yes, ma'am," I answered, being extra polite like the social worker told me.

"Come. Let me have a look at you," she said. She pushed my scruffy blonde bangs out of my face and squeezed my shoulder. "Kinda scrawny, ain't you?"

"I'm strong," I said, jutting my chin out. "And I can work hard. And the lady in the car said you're my blood so you gotta take me in."

"She did, did she?" Granny asked, clickin' her dentures and rockin' back and forth. "Well, you got a bit of fire in you. That'll count for somethin'." She turned and made her way up the sagging back steps to the back door. "Well, come on then."

I nodded, relieved that we'd come to an understandin'. I inched around the kitten's carcass and the chunks of half-chewed waffles, and Granny cackled. "You ain't afraid of dead things are you?" When I didn't answer, she shrugged. "We already have one cat. It keeps the mice away just fine. No need for another mouth to feed." I wondered if my mouth would prove too much of a burden to feed, but I didn't dare ask. Instead, I followed her into the house, my plastic bag thumpin' against my leg as I climbed the steps.

Granny put me to work right away. She said if she had to feed me and patch my clothes I'd better earn my keep. I remembered the kitten, and I took her at her word. Every day I was expected to make breakfast, wash the dishes, and make the beds. I helped with laundry and ran it through the wringer. I had to get the clothes on the line before the sun was overhead. Granny hated doin' laundry. She said the soap made her eyes water.

My afternoons were spent trying to coax life out of the powder-dry soil. I scratched up whatever withered potatoes or carrots I could from the garden, then I helped with supper. The bulk of the chores fell to me, because Granny was tending to Papa Joe.

Papa Joe wasn't really my papa, and I'm not even sure his name was Joe, but that was what everyone called him. Papa Joe came around a few years before. Granny hired him to patch a hole in the roof, and he never left. At first he stayed in his car. After a while, he moved into room over the garage. By the time I came around, he was stayin' in Granny's room.

Papa Joe walked around in his undershirt and picked at his teeth with a toothpick then chewed on the soggy bit of wood for hours afterwards. Granny

Horror

said he was a "man's man," but I just thought he was lazy and had bad breath and stared at me so much it made my skin crawl. I didn't much care, though, so long as he stayed away from me. And he did, for a while.

Granny went into town a couple times a month. She didn't drive much, so if the weather was bad she had to catch a ride with Mrs. Reynolds from down the road. Mrs. Reynolds always smelled of lavender, and she kept lemon drops in her purse and passed a few to me each time she came for a visit. She never came over when Papa Joe was around, though. Granny said they were like oil and water and only a fool would waste time trying to get 'em to mix.

Mrs. Reynolds came around on Sundays on her way home from church. Papa Joe went down to The TeePee Lounge on Sundays. The sign said "closed," but the regulars knew that the backdoor was left unlocked. They'd slip in and throw back a couple of drinks and wash away their false sense of sanctity before heading home.

One Sunday, about a month after I'd arrived, Mrs. Reynolds came around for her normal visit. Granny went in to make some iced tea and told me to entertain our company, so I was doin' my best by pickin' out songs with two fingers on Granny's old upright.

After I had finished a song or two, Mrs. Reynolds called me over. "Child," she said, "I gotta ask you something, and I want to keep this all just between us, do you hear?" I wiped my nose with the back of my hand and nodded. She dug in her purse and pulled out a handkerchief with pale pink needlework around the edge. I didn't want to blow my nose and spoil the crisp white cloth, but Mrs. Reynolds was watchin' and waitin,' so it only seemed polite.

"There now," she said with a smile. "That's better." Then she passed me a few lemon drops. I counted them out and put one in my mouth and four in my pocket.

"Honey," she said as she glanced at the kitchen door, "has your Papa Joe ever… said anything to you? Maybe touched you? Or scared you?"

I looked at her kind blue eyes and tried to decide what she wanted to hear. When I didn't answer right away, she pursed her lips and tried again. "Has he ever…*done* anything? Or *tried* to do anything? You can tell me."

I wanted to answer but nothing seemed to come out. My mind went blank under those blue eyes. All I could think of was lavender and lemon drops, and the longer I waited to answer, the bluer her eyes seemed to get. She leaned closer to me, and her breath seemed to catch. I opened my mouth to try to speak. She nodded her head up and down just a little. I don't know if it was supposed to be a hint or to reassure me, but I was about to nod back at her when Granny walked in.

"Everything okay in here?" she asked.

"Oh, fine. Just fine. Junie was just keepin' me company," Mrs. Reynolds said, and a smile broke across her face like sunshine. "Oh, my! That tea looks refreshing, Enid. On a hot day like this, it's a treat."

And the moment was gone. Mrs. Reynolds and Granny started talkin' about the weather, and how the prices down at Claude's Food Mart were criminal, and how Mrs. Swineholler was an old pig herself—the way she was carryin' on with Mr. Kinderson and thinkin' no one noticed. And among all their chatter, no one noticed me. No one noticed when I slipped out and into the backyard to get away from their clickin' dentures and sweat beaded brows. They didn't notice that Papa Joe was back early from the TeePee.

I didn't notice either. He must've been watchin' me for a few minutes, though. Long enough for me to pet that mangy old mama cat that hung around and ate the field mice, and long enough for me to wonder why Mrs. Reynolds seemed all nervous and whispery when she asked me about Papa Joe. I was thinkin' so hard that I never saw him standin' in the shadows by the garage—not until he grabbed me from behind and pulled me inside. One hand locked onto my shoulder and the other hand clamped over my mouth. I guess he didn't want me to scream, but I didn't even think to open my mouth. I should 've kicked him or bit him. I should've done *anything* other than let him drag me into that garage. Once he got me in the shadows, he pushed me up against the old steamer trunks stacked against the wall so hard that the lid bounced open and closed, lettin' out a waft of stale air that reeked of mildew.

In his eagerness, his sweaty palm kept slippin' from my mouth, but I still didn't scream. For a second, I wondered if this was how Mama felt—that day in the motel before she died—with that sweaty man on top of her breathin' heavy. He didn't even notice that she was cryin'. He was too busy rockin' back and forth and gruntin' like a pig.

Papa Joe didn't notice I was cryin' either. In fact, I didn't really notice it until later. I should've been trying to figure out how to make him stop, but instead I kept thinkin' about Mama. I didn't mean to do that to Papa Joe, but I didn't try to stop it, either. It was all over with before I even had time to think straight—just like at the motel. One minute Papa Joe was gropin' at me, tuggin' at my shorts, breathin' real loud in my ear, and the next minute he was crumpled on the floor with a knot on the back of his head the size of an egg. When he put his hands on me, he flew back and hit the wall then slid down limp and bloodied—crumpled up like that kitten by the trashcan.

Papa Joe rubbed at his oozing scalp and winced. "Keep your mouth shut and

Horror

maybe I won't tell your Granny you got the demon in you." He struggled to his feet, but kept his distance, the way you keep away from a dog that nipped at you. "I don't know what kind of monster you are, child, but they don't take kindly to demons and devils 'round here. 'Specially your Granny. She's a God-fearing woman."

I just wished he would shut up so I could think, so I could try to understand how he ended up bloodied on the floor and how come my skin felt jittery and my hair was standin' on end, and why it all seemed so…familiar.

"Keep your mouth shut, and maybe you can stay," he said, inching closer. I closed my eyes to try to stop the poundin' that was growin' in my head. I could feel him drawin' closer, I could feel where he was—just like I could feel a shadow when it blocked the sun—and when Papa Joe came too close, his voice still jabberin' and pricklin' at my throbbin' head, I yelled, "Stop!"

He didn't though. I guess he thought a ten year old wasn't much of a threat. Maybe whatever urge made him want to pull down my pants was stronger than the urge to keep himself safe. Or maybe he just thought I looked small and scared, like that little kitten, and when I thought of its crumbled body I felt the anger swell again and I felt all jittery. Then the shadow was gone.

When opened my eyes, Papa Joe was flat on his back. Blood trickled from the corner of his mouth; his eyes were closed.

I walked closer. I wondered if he was fakin'—if this was some trick. But the bloody tooth on the ground next to him told me that he wasn't foolin'. I crept forward and snatched it, wiped it on my shorts, then tucked it in my pocket with the lemon drops—my hands still shakin'. I thought it would be best if I left before he woke up.

Mrs. Reynolds was gone when I went inside. Granny was mutterin' under her breath and peelin' potatoes at the kitchen table and getting nearly as many peelings on the floor as in the trashcan.

"People need to mind their own business," she said, wavin' her paring knife at me. "What goes on in a person's house ain't no one else's business. They best tend their own garden before they come around tellin' me how to tend mine."

Granny didn't ask why my shorts were smeared with blood, and I didn't offer. Lookin' back, this must have been the start of things. The start of the lies—and of my collectin'.

When I slipped in the tiny bedroom under the attic where I slept, I pulled the tooth out of my pocket. It was yellowing and had a dark hole bore into it, but it was my first souvenir so I wanted to keep it safe. I tugged a sock from the bottom drawer of my bureau and slipped the tooth inside, then I balled the

sock back up before tuckin' it towards the back of the drawer.

Papa Joe never told Granny Enid why he showed up on the back steps bloody that day, and she never asked. She must've figured he had a scuffle over at the TeePee. At any rate, Papa Joe didn't come near me again for a while.

The next day was Monday, which meant a long walk into town to get groceries. Mrs. Reynolds couldn't drive us 'cause she was off doin' some kind of work with some girls that got themselves in some kinda trouble. Granny had a car, but she didn't get a chance to drive it much—Papa Joe always kept the car for himself. He said he needed it to look for a job, but the only lookin' he did was for his next drink. He'd drive down to the TeePee and drink until it was time to come home for supper. Granny never said a word though, not even today when the clouds were heavy with rain and the thunder grumbled. She called it "holding her tongue."

I could tell by the way she clicked her dentures that holding her tongue didn't come real natural to her, but that day Granny held her tongue tighter than she held my hand as she pulled me along the red dirt road that winded towards town. My worn shoes kicked up a cloud of rust colored dust as I struggled to keep up with her, but she was too busy eying the heavy clouds to notice.

I would've asked her to slow down, but it was too muggy to even talk. The heat sucked the words right out of your head before your mouth could even form them. So we walked on, cutting through the thick, humid air.

The click of her dentures matched the pattering of our feet as we tried to beat the storm. I wished Granny would stop at Claude's Food Mart, just this once, instead of walkin' the extra half mile to Reyn-Rite Grocery. She wouldn't though. I knew because the one time I dared ask, she said she'd rather waste a few steps than waste her money at a store run by a no-good philanderer. So, I didn't bother to ask again.

When we finally turned onto Main Street, the first heavy drops of water plopped onto the hard earth and swelled up into rusty beads of moisture. They reminded me of the drops of blood that Papa Joe left on the garage floor yesterday. I shivered a little when I thought about it. I might've thought about it more, but a low rumble shook the ground, followed by a crash of lightning that shook me out of my thoughts. Granny let go of my hand, raised her pocket book over her head, and abandoned me for the promise of shelter.

I caught up with her just as she tugged open the door to Reyn-Rite. The bell overhead jangled, but it was drowned out by a screech of laughter.

Horror

"Land sakes, Johnny," a familiar voice crooned, "I had no idea that you were so clever!" I left Granny's side and followed the velvety voice deeper into the store, eager to see who would dare address Mr. Reynolds in such a familiar way. I had never even heard Mrs. Reynolds call him anything other than "Mr. Reynolds" or "my husband."

But it wasn't Mrs. Reynolds. I could tell that even from behind. She would never wear a skirt so short, or peroxide her hair, or allow someone to touch her like that. No, Mrs. Reynolds was a proper lady. Dottie Swineholler, though, she wasn't proper. Grannie and Mrs. Reynolds whispered about that nearly every time they had coffee together. They were right.

Mrs. Swineholler and Mr. Reynolds were standin' near the candy counter just smilin' and laughin' so much that they never even noticed us. Giant jars of sweets surrounded them, every temptation imaginable, and behind them was the treat that Mrs. Reynolds's passed me when no one was lookin'—bright yellow lemon drops.

Just the sight of Mr. Reynolds's hand on the swell of that ugly cow's hip made me shake. My heart felt too tight, and it thumped hard and fast in my chest. My hair stood on end and crackled like it did when I brushed it too much when the air was dry. My fingers felt full and swollen, and everything around me got dark until all I could see was Mr. Reynolds leaning forward to whisper something in Mrs. Swineholler's ear. She pulled back, actin' all shy, which was a big lie and—just then—thunder cracked, and lightning must have struck close by because the whole room lit up.

I guess I fell backwards, 'cause when I sat up I was surrounded by lemon drops rollin' around on the floor. Mr. Reynolds's was screamin' and clawin' at his face with his hands. He clawed so hard that he knocked his glasses clean off his face, and they slid across the floor and sent more lemon drops rolling.

At first, Mrs. Swineholler didn't say a word though, she was just starin' at the splatters of red all over her fancy white dress. She didn't even seem to notice the bits of glass stickin' out of her cheek. "My dress! My dress!" she finally screamed. Like anyone gave a rat's fart about her dress.

Granny rounded the corner of the aisle and nearly slid on the lemon drops, but she righted herself. She reached a hand down and jerked me off the floor, glancin' over me. "You hurt, child?" she asked.

"No, ma'am," I said, shakin' my head. I still wasn't sure quite what happened, but something made me want to be very polite so I could go back to bein' ignored.

Granny stared at the giant jar of lemon drops—or what was left of it. Big shards of glass were stuck in the wall, and tiny bits glittered on the dusty wood

floor like diamonds. Other jagged bits had found their way into the soft flesh of Mr. Reynolds and Mrs. Swineholler. Served 'em right, if you ask me.

Granny must've thought so too, because once she saw the smear of Mrs. Swineholler's bright pink lip stick on Mr. Reynolds's cheek, right next to the red splatters, she turned and marched from the store.

"Junie Rae, we gotta find ourselves a new store. This one ain't fit for proper people," she said, and I started to follow her. Mrs. Swineholler called after us—first askin' for help, then callin' us some names that I wasn't allowed to repeat, but none of it swayed Granny's heart. I stopped though. The crunch of glass under my feet fell silent, and all that was left was their snifflin' and cryin'.

Then I crouched down and picked up the broken pair of glasses, and I tucked them into my pocket before catchin' up with Granny.

I don't know if Granny ever told Mrs. Reynolds what we saw or not. Mrs. Reynolds still came around the house, but she didn't offer me any more lemon drops after that. Truth is, I kinda lost my taste for them.

For a while after that, there were just little secrets. I found out that Granny hid money in the coffee tin over the ice box. Then I found out that wasn't really much of a secret, because Papa Joe knew about it and helped himself to it regularly.

I found out that Mrs. Reynolds was gettin' divorced, and even though some people in town thought it made her a bad person, Granny just said that people needed to tend to their own garden and quit worryin' so much about everyone else's.

I also saw Mrs. Hayne feedin' a stray cat, even though her husband kept trying to run it off. So the next time Papa Joe said it was a good thing God gave her money because He was sure stingy in the looks department, it made my heart tight.

This time I was able to close my eyes and take a few deep breaths, like I kinda' remembered Mama tryin' to teach me once, and then my hair quit cracklin' and my heart eased up. Later, though, when he told me to get off my lazy backside and get him a beer, I made sure to spit it in a few times before I took it to him.

After what happened at the store, Granny seemed to have a lot more chores for me around the house, so I didn't get to go into town much. Sometimes I caught her lookin' at me funny then turnin' away real fast.

Mrs. Reynolds still came by for coffee, though, so I didn't get too lonely. It was during one of her visits that I learned the start of a secret that would change everything.

Horror

"I was over at the Curl & Cut getting my hair set, and Virginia Hershell said that they had a new lodger check in. Said she was real pretty. Young, too," she said as she added a splash of milk to her coffee. Then she frowned. "You can bet Mr. Reynolds will be around to welcome her. Might be best if we head over to greet her soon—tip her off—for her own good, you know."

Granny's brows scrunched together and she nodded. "Hate for her to get off on the wrong foot, being new to the town and all. Did Virginia give you her name?"

"No, but she said that the lady was some sort of social worker—here on a home visit, or some such."

I wondered if it was the same lady who drove me here and bought me waffles. I quit pickin' at my fingers and looked over at Granny, but I didn't dare ask. Granny looked pale and nervous, but Mrs. Reynolds didn't seem to notice, she just kept talkin' and sippin' her coffee. "Virginia said she only paid for a couple of days. 'Course that's plenty enough time for Mr. Reynolds to get into—"

"Land sakes, look at the time!" Granny said, cutting Mrs. Reynolds off. "I best get supper on before Papa Joe gets home."

"Oh, dear. Look at me, just carryin' on. I'll come around tomorrow, and we can drive into town and drop by Virginia's place. Maybe get us a cherry Coke while we are there," Mrs. Reynolds said, walking towards the door.

"That'll be real fine," Granny said, rushing around Mrs. Reynolds to get the door for her. "You have yourself a good evenin' now."

Granny seemed distracted afterwards. I wanted to ask why the social worker had come back, but Granny kept givin' me chores to do. Turns out, I didn't have to wait long.

Granny had just put the pot roast on when there was a knock at the front door. Granny wiped her hands on her apron, then untied it and hung it on a hook by the stove before makin' her way to the front door. She waved me away, then she opened the door with a smile bigger than any I'd ever seen her face make before.

Well, I wasn't gonna miss out on that, so I tucked myself behind Papa Joe's recliner just as Granny pushed open the squeaky screen. I tried to make my breathing quieter, but then my heart just seemed to beat louder. So I held my breath as long as I could, so I'd catch every word.

"Come on in then, Miss Jones," Granny said. "I heard you were in town."

"I'm afraid so," she said. "I got word that there have been some troubles around here."

"Troubles? I don't know nothin' about no troubles. Everything's been just fine. Right as rain," Granny said, clickin' her teeth. "Have a seat. Can I get you some coffee?" Granny didn't bother to sit down.

Miss Jones passed over Papa Joe's sweat stained recliner and took Granny's rocker nearer to the door. "Nothing for me, thanks. I should just get right to it. When we brought June here, we had hoped that things would be kept… discreet," Miss Jones said, her voice crisp and sharp—not all smooth and soft like when she delivered me here. "That is why we are paying you such a handsome sum—for your discretion."

"Well, I ain't said a word to no one," Granny replied, her voice rising. "And you best not be havin' ideas about goin' back on our agreement."

"As I recall," Miss Jones replied, "our *agreement* was for you to keep the child out of trouble and out of sight. We know of at least one public incident, which—experience shows—means there've been more. It's simply not acceptable. She'll have to be placed with another foster. I'm here to collect her."

"Junie's blendin' in real nice here. She ain't done nothin' wrong, so you can just turn your fancy car around and go back where you came from. You won't be collectin' no one," Granny said, marchin' over and openin' the door real wide.

"Where is she?" Miss Jones asked. "I'll gather her things and we'll be out of here. You'll be compensated for your troubles, of course. You're lucky, really. You should have seen what the girl did to her mother before we took charge of her. There is a reason people like that can't be running wild—we have to protect normal folk."

"Out!" Granny said, her voice quivering.

"Just hand her over, you old fool!" Miss Jones said, grabbing Granny by the arm and shaking her.

Then suddenly, *everything* seemed to be shaking, and my hair crackled and rose around me like the halos I saw in the Bible at church. I didn't feel like an angel, though. I felt angry and mighty, and I wanted to hurt that lady that was makin' Granny cry. I wanted to hurt her like I hurt Papa Joe when he grabbed me, like I hurt that man who was on top of Mama makin' her cry in the hotel room.

So I did.

I closed my eyes, and I shared my secret.

When I opened my eyes, all that was left of Miss Jones was a dark shadow on the wall, and a bent hair pin—dark and charred—on the floor. Seemed I'd gotten better at sharin' my secret than I was that day at the hotel. I closed my eyes and tried not to remember. Some things are best locked away. That's what they told me when they collected me the first time.

Granny came over and helped me up, smoothed down my singed hair, and led me into the kitchen. Then she tied on her apron, filled a bucket with water,

Horror

grabbed an old rag, and disappeared into the living room for a while. When she came back, the water was nearly black and her hands were covered in soot. She untied her apron and passed it to me as she nodded towards the laundry basket on the table.

I patted the apron pockets down, just like Granny taught me to do, before I added it to the pile of dirty clothes. Inside the folds of the apron was a dark twisted bit of metal with melted plastic pearls. The hair pin. I slid it in my pocket then turned back towards Granny.

She washed up without a word, but her hands shook as she checked on the pot roast. "This never happened. Do you hear me, Junie Rae? This is our secret."

I nodded my head, and she smiled, then she rummaged in the cabinet and dug out a stale cookie from a tin of leftover Christmas cookies. I took it from her before she changed her mind.

"We should take a trip to town tomorrow," Granny said, settling herself at the kitchen table. "I reckon its time someone visited Dottie Swineholler and set her straight on a few things. Might stop and see Mr. Reynolds, too, while we are at it. He has some things to account for as well." She rattled off a list of names for a good long while, and the shadows snuck in while she talked, but she didn't bother to turn on the lights. I figured that was as good a time as any to help myself to a few more cookies.

We were still sittin' at the kitchen table when Papa Joe came home. The pot roast was cooked to a dry lump, and the sun had long since sunk beneath the red-tinged hills. He always seemed to stumble in smellin' of cigarettes and beer and cheap perfume, and I figured tonight wouldn't be any exception. My nose crinkled in anticipation.

When Granny had taught me how to wash clothes, she'd smelled Papa Joe's shirts before she shoved them in the wash water. Then she'd dabbed at her eyes. She said the soap made her eyes water.

Granny stood up when she heard him clammerin' up the back steps. She clicked her teeth and folded her arms. Papa Joe slammed open the backdoor. He brought with him the smell of sweat, and beer, and unwashed bedding. He didn't seem to notice me. He stumbled right towards Granny. He buried his face in her neck and breathed in the smell of her while she tried to untangle herself from him, but he wouldn't let go. He just kept tellin' her how she looked mighty fine and how nothin' else meant anything, really. Then he shoved her against the cabinet and pushed himself up against her. It reminded me of what happened to Mama in the hotel room, and it made my hair crackle and my heart gallop. I looked up at Granny, expectin' her to shake her head, or holler at me to go away.

But instead she just smiled at me, kinda sad like.

Then she closed her eyes, took a deep breath, and pushed at Papa Joe with all her might. "Wait, Joe. Hold on—Junie has a secret to share with you…"

Papa Joe stumbled backwards, his arms spread wide like an invitation.

Granny nodded her head. I opened my hand and let the last of the Christmas cookie fall to the floor, and I added him to my collection.

The End

Terri Wallace lives in Oklahoma with her husband, three children, and a menagerie of cats, dogs, and chickens. When she isn't busy gardening or re-reading Outlander, she can be found writing strange stories and blogging at https://TerriZellerWallace.wordpress.com.

He Walks in My Black

By Paul Draper

"When I close my eyes he walks," said the old French woman. She'd said she was eighty but her eyes looked many times that age. "When I open them, he stops. He's walked my whole life, starting in the sea when I was just a girl. I saw his eyes, you see."

I listened to this frail, rambling lady in the sunny square as I swapped my punctured tyre over at the village cafe. She'd been talking to herself when I'd arrived and ordered my drink, but now seemed to be addressing me.

"They'll not see me again," she looked across the square at the local villagers milling about, then turned to gaze beyond the village sign to the forest. "He's in the trees now." She stood and hobbled in that direction, southward down the lane.

It took a while to pack up, but by early afternoon I'd glided out of the village and was steadily climbing south towards Monpartre.

My spirits were high as I cycled on through the Pyrenean ascent. I felt like I was travelling towards a new me, a better version on the horizon. The June sun glanced from the peaks and I took it easy on the climb, which curved round to keep the valley I was leaving in view. I'd stopped to take on water and soak in the panorama when my phone softly buzzed. The caller ID was *Carl P – London Clinic*. I wiped the sweat from my hands and answered.

"Hi Carl."

"Morning Ben. Well you sound relaxed. All going ok?" he asked in his usual reassuring tone.

"Pretty knackering, but yep all good."

"I'm proud of you. You wouldn't have pictured yourself doing that this time last year!"

Smiling, I thought about the year we'd shared; the nerves and the rows, the fear of even stepping out of the car and into the open street. "Bloody right I wouldn't. I'm bang on schedule though."

"Well, take it easy and look after yourself. I'm here if you need me, but still ok for a daily check-in?"

"Yes, for sure. Thanks again for all your help."

I briefly thought about texting Dawn a photo, me smiling outdoors on an adventure. *Look what I'm doing! I'm better!*

Like I'd ever send such a thing. She would probably be on her own adventures now, free from all my crap.

I packed the bottle and phone back into the saddlebag and rode on.

In the approaching dusk I stopped at the head of the valley to check the map, as it wouldn't pay to take the wrong route over the ridge. The view was bright and clear for the time of day. At that moment I caught a movement from the corner of my vision. It was a vast figure striding across the wooded valley floor, way below.

I struggled to make sense of the perspective but saw the shape of a man of enormous size. He sported what appeared to be either a wide hat or horns and was easily the height of the nearby mature trees.

I saw a cottage beyond, directly in his path. Smoke rose in the chimney, but there were no lamps lit. He walked towards it with a strained and leaning gait, like that of a bull pulling a plough.

The surrounding mountains looked on impassively. I felt an overpowering urge to be clear of this valley as soon as possible.

My thighs strained as I pulled the bike clear of the valley ascent and approached the junction forking off and leading to a slight descent on the other side. I heard a faint sound from the valley I was leaving; a splintering and cracking as if trees were being felled. I couldn't resist a final glance back.

What I saw then haunts me as I lay here now.

The cottage had been completely destroyed. Smoke drifted across the remaining timbers in the increasing gloom and the giant figure stood in the centre, apparently stamping hard onto something in the ruins, before bending down to scoop whatever it was into its mouth. A deep call, like the lowing of a ship's horn in fog, carried in the gentle breeze and the figure looked up.

Looked at me.

Horror

The distance between us must have been approaching a kilometre, but I have no doubt that the dark pits resembling eyes in the figure's face swivelled directly to lock onto mine. He cocked his head as if listening for something, before turning to face me full on. His gaze seemed to push effortlessly past my eyes to paint the back of my skull. The breeze whipped around my ears and a single word came to mind, as if the air itself had boiled and formed the sound; *prochain*.

Despite being high and in all reason safe from reach, I recoiled and my ankle clattered against the pedal arm as I groped to find purchase on the bike. Before starting off I shut my eyes for a few seconds. Upon opening them I could see he had strode about twenty yards towards me and settled to a stop.

I pressed hard on the pedals and restarted the climb, looking back over my shoulder just before the valley curved out of view.

Head still angled up, he had not moved a single step further.

With the cycle lights on, my descent to Monpartre was a jumble of thoughts and a strain to make sense of what I had seen. An hour later I arrived at the *auberge* I'd marked in the itinerary and was devouring soup and crusty bread. Fatigue started to take its toll.

Despite my tiredness it was a while before sleep claimed me that night. The single word *prochain* played on a loop. It meant 'next'; what was next?

When sleep came, it was fitful and carried dreams laced with slamming steps and the smell of burning meat. All the while I heard a steady deep rhythm, a metronomic crunching of rubble and sticks. I was faintly aware of that old, familiar rising anxiety that stifled the breath in my throat and eventually jarred me awake at dawn, tense and aching.

My command of French wasn't advanced enough to adequately describe the previous day's events at breakfast, and my host had a brusque Gallic air about him that didn't encourage conversation. Mute and frustrated, I eventually decided the best thing to do would be to get down to a few more days riding and try as best I could to leave the uncanny events in that valley behind. A night's sleep had rationalised some of it – odd light perspectives in the gloaming, maybe the dusky evening water vapour had magnified sounds and sights. I had been convinced about the destruction of the cottage, but then perhaps in moving further up the valley I had revealed another, ruined, cottage to my view and had confused the two. Perhaps I'd witnessed a folk tradition or play of some kind.

Those darkened eyeholes though.

I made twenty five miles before late afternoon and as my stomach called for fuel I wheeled down a steady decline to rest at a roadside tavern called *Le Coq Bleu*.

It was basic but pleasant and I loaded up my carbs with a plate of Toulouse sausages *avec frites* then gave Carl a call. I told him briefly about the previous day's weirdness, trying not to sound like too much of a nutter. Between us we'd already dealt with enough.

"Perhaps it was a local custom or something?"

"Yes, I thought that. Perhaps…probably."

"How about the anxiety levels and sleep?"

I didn't want to allow that back into my life. "No, that's ok still." As we spoke I watched three children playing in the adjacent yard with an old ball. Two of the three were playing at least, as the third, a boy of about ten, seemed intent on just observing me like a zoo exhibit. I pulled a face. He continued staring.

"It's a big test you're taking, so remember to keep to the rest stops, and you can always stay on for a day or two in one place and get some rest."

We signed off and I stared back at the boy. "*Bonjour*," I said.

The boy just looked at me – or rather looked just above my head. He slowly walked a few steps towards me and said simply, "*Vous avez le signe.*" He turned and walked off.

I later saw the boy, presumably the innkeeper's son, talking in hushed tones with his father. Later, the stout man showed me my room, explaining gruffly that it was only available for one night.

That night was even more restless than the previous one.

In my dream I could smell an acrid and pungent curl of fur and clay. Bitter smoke settled on my tongue. Again that crunching tramp beat a slow rhythm. I could sense a shuddering of the ground across my back as I lay half in sleep and half out, a nautical rope knot of unease clasped across my chest. I drifted towards consciousness and could still feel the tiniest of vibrations beating lightly on my spine as I lay on my back in the modest cot. My mind wheeled. With my eyes open, the dream was persisting.

I opened my eyes and listened. Outside the warm Pyrenean night air sang loudly with silence. The moon shone dimly and the glow from a small tungsten lamp on the side of the inn cast a sickly light against the top of the window frame. I could feel the dampness of my pillow against my perspiring head.

Horror

It wasn't that hot. Maybe I was ill.

I closed my eyes to again reach for sleep and the hairs on my neck beat a slow tattoo against the mattress. My pulse? A woozy thought swam forward; perhaps at the next town I should try to find a doctor.

Pulse, pulse, went the neck hairs. Tiny mattress tremors in the quiet still air.

Sleep rose up to latch my attention with gently tugging silk strings, yet a small voice whispered on a loop.

Don't sleep.

Pulse, pulse, pulse.

Something comes.

The echo of that phrase pursued my mind down to slumber's edge, where my consciousness took it, turned it over and looked at it with a sleepy but analytical eye. Within a few seconds I was as awake as I'd ever been.

Something comes.

I dressed hurriedly and clambered down the steps from my room and out of the front door. Fat, woozy insects dinged mindlessly against the inn's fixed coach-lamp as I took a few steps across the dusty forecourt and peered northward along the road.

The side of the hill was strewn in moonlight, the higher sides of rocks and trees gilded with silver. There was a small copse of trees halfway up, about two hundred yards from where I stood. Rubbing my eyes, the gentle slope of the combined leaf canopy undulated across the top of the copse before ending in an odd combination of shapes. The moon ducked partially behind a cloud just as my eyes started to make sense of the shapes.

A horned figure, colossal and still, and at least fifteen metres tall.

The breeze dropped and a loud bullish snort carried in the air from the copse. My galloping blood seemed to halt and I felt my windpipe constrict like a clamp.

I wheeled around to see the white-aproned innkeeper peering out at the lower window, his face ashen and struck with terror. He moved away from the window and I heard a bolt slam across on the front door I'd exited from.

Thick cloud pushed across the moon and the night went black. Behind me a shuddering gravelly step was heard from the copse.

Running to the door, I hammered on it hard.

"Go!" shouted the innkeeper from the other side.

More heavy steps from behind. My bike was around the back.

Groping in the near dark, I felt around the side of the inn to the back yard as crunching, shaking slams crossed the road on the other side. I felt the front of the bike and with sickening recall remembered my cycle lights were in my room, along with my phone. I grabbed at my pocket and with relief felt the lock keys.

A smashing of wood and stone. Screams. It was coming directly through the building for me.

I lifted the bike away from the wall and pushed away down the lane leading from the back yard as a mass of crashing and clattering sounded from the inn. Glass, wood and yells of terror.

Somehow I blindly managed to keep on the road for a hundred yards before the clouds parted to reveal the tarmac stretching out before me. I skidded to a halt and looked back on a scene of a nightmare. The giant figure stood where my bike had been rested. Behind him a clear, rubble-strewn furrow had been torn through the inn, and by his feet there laid a mangled and white-aproned figure, limbs twisted impossibly.

I cycled by moonlight on towards dawn, deeper into the mountains using the single road on which behind me stalked a nightmare. I rested when I could but now with each closing of my eyes I felt the start of relentless marching, deep inside. How ironic I could now sleep easily after so many years of tortuous nights. I could not hope to understand the link between my sight and the giant, but it felt real and fixed; a soldering together of sense and pursuing fate. I had involuntarily made a contract back in that valley I would never comprehend.

Without maps or equipment, my disorientation grew. Lacking water and nourishment, the peaks swam before my eyes, at once connected to the sky yet revolving beneath it as I pedalled ever higher. Two nights passed, sleep only arriving as I cowered in roadside scrub and could resist no longer. At times the waning moon hid away behind cloud and it was at these times my terror grew strongest. I felt the march of the demon in my bones and the coursing of my blood.

On the third day the disaster struck that left me in my current situation. Rounding a tight hairpin on one of the rare descents and nearly insane with dehydration, I saw the rock fall rubble too late. With hard cliff to my left, I could only veer wildly right and left the road at a skidding pace, becoming unseated as the bike shot away over the edge.

Then blackness.

Horror

I don't know how long I was out. Perhaps minutes, perhaps a day.

I now find myself on a ledge, barely twenty feet across. Above me is an incline over which I fell. It's too steep to climb, but I can see the road and hope for a car or perhaps workmen from Monpartre to arrive to clear the rockfall. Way below me is the twisted frame of the bike, broken on the rocks. My right ankle is swollen, numb and won't take my weight. My elbows are bloody with cuts.

The final pixels of sun blink down over the mountainside. I can keep my eyes open no longer. The moon is new tonight so it matters little, he will walk regardless.

As the comfortable, corrupting embrace of sleep rises towards me I feel the beat of his stride.

Pulse, pulse.

He has walked as long as the land has stood.

Pulse, pulse.

He will walk until the sun reaches out to touch the earth.

Pulse, pulse.

He walks in my black.

The End

Paul Draper is an English writer who lives on the south coast in Dorset, which is about as balmy as it gets in the UK. He writes in both prose and screenplay format and has won the odd local film-making award that he doesn't generally like to talk about, as well as having some sketch material shot by the BBC.

Writing mainly in dark fiction, sci-fi and comedy, if there is a consistent theme it's generally that things don't end well for his main characters, which he really ought to chat through with a counsellor at some point.

Influences are M.R. James, H.P. Lovecraft, J.S. le Fanu, and most other ghost and horror writers with two initials ahead of the surname.

Granny Mabel

By Danielle C Allen

Joshua knew he shouldn't do it, but he couldn't resist. It was just too easy. Granny Mabel sat in her garden, snoring a little, back door wide open. She was a tiny woman who wasn't any trouble, always kind to the neighbours, bought sweets for the trick-or-treaters and carol singers. She hadn't done anything to him. *Well, she is a bit weird.* Joshua thought about the last time he'd seen her, and his mind conjured up a vague memory. Granny Mabel on his door step, telling his mother she could have the broth that she cooked with the meat her son brought every month. 'I can't eat it all, and you have a growing boy to feed. Please take it, I hate to see it go to waste.' His Mother smiled and thanked her, kissing her on a hollow, wrinkled cheek. She hobbled down the path, giggling and muttering to herself.

He sat and stared over the fence at her for half an hour, remembering her generosity, then decided it was now or never. Climbing over, he sneaked past the sleeping woman, stopping for a terrifying second while she smacked her lips and shifted a little. Joshua crept into the dark house. Granny Mabel had drawn all of the curtains. The heat was almost unbearable, and it smelled of sickly sweet flowers. Joshua took his time. The woman was old and frail, if she caught him, he could easily get away. He smiled to himself as he searched her home for trinkets. The dim hallway held nothing of interest, so he started looking in the front room. Dusty ornaments lay on every surface. A large wooden box in the darkest corner caught his eye. He opened it, disturbing the layer of grey on top. It was full of teeth.

He remembered the box his mother kept in her wardrobe with his baby teeth. Shivering a little, he closed it and put it back, knocking a vase with his hand. Joshua's chest tightened as it wobbled on the shelf before coming to rest. Half

Horror

a dozen dead rosebuds fell from brown stalks and scattered. Sighing, Joshua left the front room and went to search the small kitchen. It was almost bare. A huge metal pot sat on the hob, liquid bubbling inside. The drawers had a few wooden utensils in but nothing else.

Joshua decided she must hide the good stuff upstairs, so he crept up there, each creaky step that he took calling out to the sleeping Granny in the vegetable patch. He held the banister and felt his hand rise and fall where the wood had warped and swelled. Meandering through the uneven doorways of three bedrooms and an en-suite bathroom, he found nothing of interest. Blankets and porcelain dolls. Dust bunnies under giant four poster beds that he would need a ladder to climb onto.

Joshua was about to give up, when he spotted a yellowed string hanging from the ceiling. Jumping up to reach it, he caught hold of it on his third try and pulled it with him as he landed. A section of the ceiling came away and a flap opened, metal ladders descending to his feet. He'd found the loft hatch.

Joshua looked down the stairs at the light shining in. The back door was still open, and Granny Mabel was still asleep. *Good.* He climbed the ladder and felt for the light. His fingers found a switch and he pushed it, illuminating the space. Stacked around the outside walls were hundreds of picture frames. Walking over to a big box to his left, Joshua opened it and peered inside. It rattled a little and as he bent over to see what was there, a huge brown rat shot out at him, scuttling away. Falling back and landing on his rump, Joshua held his chest and waited for the pounding in his ears to stop. *Not scared of em anyway.*

Scrambling up off the floor, he brushed the dust from his pants and went back to the box. He kicked it and waited for the noise of more rats. Wiping his sweating hands on his front, Joshua pulled the cardboard lid open and leant over to see what it held. It was filled with frames. They were bright, white, strange shapes. He picked the top one up and gasped, dropping it as he realised what it was made of. Bones. Shining white bones screwed together at the corners. Long thick bones and smaller ones, all stuck together in a pattern.

He stood for a few minutes looking down at it, then picked it up and turned it over in his hands, letting out a cautious laugh. *Fake.* Looking around, he counted the boxes. He sat the one he was holding back in its place and walked slowly around the room, looking at the frames mounted on the walls. They all held pictures of boys and girls. He recognised some of them. All of the photos had the word MISSING printed above them.

Walking up to the nearest one, his chest filled with dread as he recognised the photo. His best friend Johnny stared back at him, smiling and holding onto his scooter. He had disappeared just over a year ago. Joshua's eyes began to water and he dragged his gaze away, inspecting the others. There was Katie, who disappeared two months before Johnny, and Kenneth, who ran away before that. More and more pictures of his friends and others from school who had gone missing. Joshua trembled as his mind ticked. Granny Mabel had made all of the posters and helped put them up every time a child went missing.

Joshua decided it was time to leave. The faces of missing children burned into his eyelids. *Need some air. Need to get out.* He'd get into trouble but decided he needed to tell someone about Granny's weird stash. As he turned to leave, a strong hand grabbed his shoulder. Spinning round to see who had caught him, his eyes found Granny Mabel. She was only a few inches taller than he was, and he would easily outgrow her within the year. She smiled her sweet smile and held him in her iron grip.

'Hello dear, admiring my picture frames are you?'

Joshua tried to step back and put some space between them but she held her grip and grinned, waiting for a reply. 'Erm, yeah. Thought I heard a noise and… erm…they're nice. Really strange.'

Joshua prayed that his mumbled excuse would hold up and forced himself to smile back. His arm was starting to tingle from the pressure of her pushing down on him. She refused to let go, instead shoving him back further into the attic and blocking his escape route.

'I made them myself dear, wanted to sell them, but they make people nervous. Do they make you nervous, Joshua?' She tilted her head at an angle, like a wolf considering its options.

Joshua coughed quietly and pasted a smile on his face. 'No, I think they're cool.' He turned to reach for one, and Granny's claws dug into him. He cried out and stumbled back, falling onto the wood floor hard enough to knock the wind out of himself.

Granny Mabel advanced, her left hand wrapped around a long walking stick, her right extended to catch him if he ran. Joshua scrambled back towards the wall and wheezed. 'I…I…I'm sorry Granny Mabel, I won't do it again, I promise!' He raised his arms to shield himself as she brought the stick down on top of him as hard as she could…

…Mabel battered the little intruder lying on her attic floor until he stopped moving and blood trickled from his head. She smiled, proud of her efforts. She

Horror

knew when she'd seen him peeking over the fence that he was planning a little thieving operation while she 'slept'. Mabel loved moments like that, when she knew she would be adding to the collection.

She dragged his limp body to the edge of the attic door and pushed him out of the hole in the floor. He landed with a thud at the bottom of the ladder and she followed, turning off the light as she went. Pushing the attic door back up, ladder and all, she grabbed the boy by the leg and pulled him down the stairs, his thick head making a sound like hollow wood as it hit each step. The pan in the kitchen was ready for him.

Removing his clothes, Granny Mabel attached him to the ropes waiting on the bench and lifted him from the floor, pulley wheels squeaking as they rattled along the ceiling. She lowered him into the boiling water, and the pan sizzled as it filled to the top with its added ingredient. Rubbing her hands together, she went to sit in the front room and admire her ornaments while the broth cooked.

She picked up the first one on the shelf and blew the dust away, turning it over in her hands. This had been her first one. A tiny ankle, toes taken off and stowed in the attic with the rest. She lifted it to her face and drank in the smell of bone. She pressed her thin lips to the ankle, kissing it. Putting it back on the shelf, she took each one of the bones in turn and swept away the dust.

Three hours later, the broth was ready, and she went to the kitchen to take out the meat. Scooping the heavy load from the huge pan, she clonked Joshua's carcass down on the bench with a thud. Only the sharpest knife in the block would do for this job. She grabbed it and began to slice, pulling the tender flesh from his bones and throwing it into a bowl.

When she had got the last of the meat off, she filled the sink, putting the skeleton in there to soak. The biggest slices of meat were put to one side and the rest she chopped and put back into the pan of stock, adding some lentils and potatoes. She left that to boil and set to work on the bones. Washing them a bit at a time, she pulled the hand and arm apart at the wrist and placed them on the drying rack. She continued to dismantle the boy and stack him neatly to her left. *He will make an excellent frame.*

Granny Mabel gathered him up and hobbled to the attic, placing his pieces carefully on the floor and taking her drill from the tool box. She arranged his pretty bones and made them into a pattern, criss crossing fingers and toes over the bigger leg and arm bones until she was happy with it. She drilled and screwed until he was whole and picked him up, holding him in front of her to admire her work. *Pretty bones.*

Stacking Joshua in the corner on his own, she went to get the posters she had printed. She took one from the pile and slotted it into the frame, holding him at arm's length to make sure he was straight. Hooking him into place next to his best friend Johnny, she smiled to herself. *Next will be the Collins boy.* Stroking the empty space on the other side of Johnny, she giggled and clapped, then went back downstairs to her broth, and hummed as she stirred...

...Mary sat at the kitchen table, sobbing quietly. She looked at the place where Joshua usually sat and anguish welled up in her chest. He had been gone for three days. None of her neighbours seemed to care. So many children had run away from here and no one had offered any comfort to mothers who put up endless posters and knocked on doors. Only Granny Mabel had offered a shoulder to cry on. She'd come as soon as the first posters went up, bringing homemade broth and a friendly ear. 'Don't worry dear, I'm sure he is just off having an adventure somewhere, not a care in the world.'

She smiled a little as she heard the familiar knock on her door and went to answer it. Granny Mabel's face stared up at her. She held out a small pan of broth and her forehead wrinkled with concern. 'You look like you haven't eaten for days, dear. I brought you some meat and potato broth, you eat up.' She pushed the pan into Mary's hands and patted her arm, then turned and hobbled down the path and across the road.

Mary took the broth to the stove to heat it up. It smelled divine. She warmed a little as she stirred her lunch. Granny Mabel had printed posters using a picture she'd taken of Joshua last year, standing with his bicycle in her garden. She'd been putting them up everywhere. Mary sat down at her empty kitchen table to eat, feeling grateful to have such a kind neighbour. She made a mental note to pop round to say thank you and wiped her tear stained face.

Granny Mabel sat on her comfy garden chair, waiting for her next visitor. She'd left the shed open just a crack, knowing that he wouldn't be able to resist the urge to explore the dark space. The large trap door in the middle was open and covered in mouldy green carpet. Hearing the rustling of her hedges to the left, she sank down and closed her eyes.

Letting her jaw drop slightly, she uttered well-practised slumber nonsense and waited. Christopher Collins peeked out of the greenery at Granny Mabel's sleeping form. He grinned and sneaked across the garden towards the open shed he'd spied earlier. Tiptoeing across, he let himself in, freezing as the door

Horror

creaked slightly.

Granny's eyes shot open as she heard the thud behind her. Mouth filling with saliva at the thought of her new project, she rose and stretched. Granny Mabel hobbled into her lair and closed the door. Hurrying down into the cellar, she clapped her hands together and squealed as the Collins boy writhed and groaned on the floor. *Yes. Pretty bones.*

The End

Danielle Allen is 28 years old and has been writing for nine years. She was born in Newcastle upon Tyne. After attending courses at Newcastle College and Sunderland University studying Music with Media, Danielle discovered her passion for writing.

She has been published on the Reader's Digest website and in their print magazine as a runner up in their 100 word story competition two years running.

She was also published on flash-fiction-world.com in November 2012 and in their fourth anthology in April 2013, and on wordriot.org in their June 15th 2013 issue, and has been a runner up in several txtlit competitions.

Danielle's short story, Robbie's Village, is now available on amazon for kindle, courtesy of Pentalpha Publishing Edinburgh. Danielle is currently working on her first novel and a collection of short horror fiction.

http://www.amazon.co.uk/gp/product/B00C5S3U52

http://www.wordriot.org/archives/5747

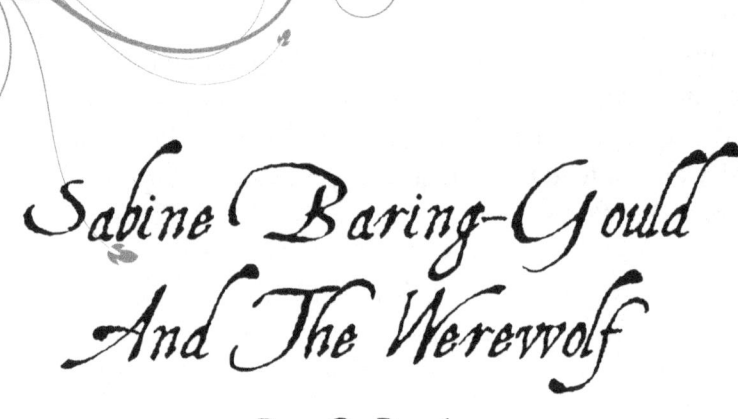

Sabine Baring-Gould And The Werewolf

Roy C. Booth

Sabine Baring-Gould and the Werewolf was first published as a cover story for Necrotic Tissue #8, October 2009, Stygian Publications.

Recently it was drawn to my attention of a letter sent out by Vicar Sabine Baring-Gould to Dr. H. Philpotts, the Bishop of Exeter. This letter, among many other of Dr. Philpott's, had recently been discovered, not in the Bishop Philpotts Library in Truro, Cornwall, but in the archives of the Devon County Library. As Dr. Philpotts at the time was in his late 80s and was harangued by the increasing agitation of his opponents for his many spurious pamphlets, this letter was among many that the Church of England had carefully archived, yet not opened.

The beginning may perhaps be familiar to the reader as it was recounted later in Baring-Gould's much larger and longer work, published in 1865 as The Book of Were-Wolves. *The letter in full has been carefully restored to the best of my ability (the original was damaged over the past 150 years or so, and I have tried to piece it all back together, but, alas, I am a historian, not a writer), and submit it now to you, the reader, in its entirety.*

Christian Royce, Historian, London, 2008.

Horror

To his Eminence the Bishop of Exeter, Dr. H. Philpotts,

I most humbly submit to you a request to review a most bizarre occurrence of the unnatural kind that had happened to me, while I was investigating a cromlech at Vienne, France this spring. It has shook me to my very essence and I must request from you assistance in understating the importance of this strange event that befell me that one fateful night.

For your perusal I have diligently copied for you the excerpt as it appears in my diary. I have kept nothing back and I have simply told the tale as it has unfolded to me.

My interest in the supernatural has been sparked by this miraculous event, and I would be most appreciative to hear what you, of your stature with and as a worldly man of your character would truthfully think of the matter. While it seems that the supernatural has been in this enlightened age relegated to the old wives tales to frighten children and simpletons, there nonetheless – I fear might be the possibility that these creatures equally do exist here in the British Isles, and that if that were to be true what manner of safeguards should be emplaced to guard our very souls.

Your ever faithful servant,

S. Baring-Gould

I shall never forget the walk I took one night in Vienne, after having accomplished the examination of an unknown Druidical relic, the Pierre labie, at La Rondelle, near Champigni. I had learned of the existence of this cromlech only on my arrival at Champigni in the afternoon, and I had started to visit the curiosity without calculating the time it would take me to reach it and to return. Suffice it to say that I discovered the venerable pile of gray stones as the sun set, and that I expended the last lights of evening in planning and sketching. I then turned my face homeward. My walk of about ten miles had wearied me, coming at the end of a long day's posting, and I had lamed myself in scrambling over some stones to the Gaulish relic.

A small hamlet was at no great distance, and I betook myself hither, in the hopes of hiring a trap to convey me to the posthouse, but I was disappointed. Few in the place would speak French, and the priest, when I applied to him, assured me that he believed there was no better conveyance in the place than a common *charrue* with its solid wooden wheels; nor was a riding horse to be procured. The good man offered to house me for the night; but I was obliged to decline, as my family intended starting early on the following morning.

Out spake then the mayor: "Monsieur can never go back tonight across the flats, because of the...the..." and his voice dropped; "the *loups-garoux*."

"He says that he must return!" replied the priest in *patois*. "But who will go with him?"

"Ah, ha! M. le Curé. It is all very well for one of us to accompany him, but think of the coming back alone!"

"Then two must go with him," said the priest, "and you can take care of each other as you return."

"Picou tells me that he saw the were-wolf only this day se'nnight," said a peasant; "he was down by the hedge of his buckwheat field, and the sun had set, and he was thinking of coming home, when he heard a rustle on the far side of the hedge. He looked over, and there stood a wolf as big as a calf against the horizon, its tongue out, and its eyes glaring like marsh-fires. Mon Dieu! Catch me going over the *marais* tonight. Why, what could two men do if they were attacked by that wolf-fiend?"

"It is tempting Providence," said one of the elders of the village; "no man must expect the help of God if he throws himself willfully in the way of danger. Is it not so, M. le Curé? I heard you say as much from the pulpit on the first Sunday in Lent, preaching from the Gospel."

"That is true," observed several, shaking their heads.

"His tongue hanging out, and his eyes glaring like marsh-fires!" said the confidant of Picou.

"Mon Dieu! If I met the monster, I should run," quoth another.

"I quite believe you, Cortrez; I can answer for it that you would," said the mayor.

"As big as a calf," threw in Picou's friend.

"If the loup-garou were only a natural wolf, why then, you see" – the mayor cleared his throat – "you see we should think nothing of it; but, M. le Curé, it is a fiend, a worse than fiend, a man-fiend – a worse than man-fiend, a man-wolf-fiend."

"But what is the young monsieur to do?" asked the priest, looking from one to another.

Horror

"Never mind," said I, who had been quietly listening to their patois, which I understood. "Never mind; I will walk back myself, and if I meet the loup-garou I will crop his ears and tail, and send them to M. le Maire with my compliments."

A sigh of relief arose from the assembly, as they found themselves clear of the difficulty.

"*Il est Anglais,*" said the mayor, shaking his head, as though he meant that an Englishman might face the devil with impunity.

A melancholy flat was the marais, looking desolate enough by day, but now, in the gloaming, tenfold as desolate. The sky was perfectly clear, and a soft, blue-gray tinge; illuminated by the new moon, a curve of light approaching its western bed. To the horizon reached a fen, blacked with pools of stagnant water, from which the frogs kept up an incessant trill through the summer night. Heath and fern covered the ground, but near the water grew dense masses of flag and bulrush, amongst which the light wind sighed wearily. Here and there stood a sandy knoll, capped with firs, looking like black splashes against the grey sky; not a sign of habitation anywhere; the only trace of men being the white, straight road extending for miles across the fen.

That this district harbored wolves was not improbable, and I confess that I armed myself with a strong stick at the first clump of trees through which the road dived.

Upon that road I set myself to walk.

The path itself became as I progressed more weed choked, and darker. The moon bringing deep shadows and brilliant highlights against a road that shone with a queer eeriness.

The sandy fens soon turned to heavier bushes as the water wound itself farther from the road. The forest fell soon silent as the bulrushes and frogs were left behind. The thicket, for that is the only way it can be called, became an impenetrable mass of sharp and thorny protrusions that would at times seem to leap against my arms seeking to scrape against the skin.

The journey itself was not difficult, but for my lame leg, which caused me first to use my strong stick not as a protection from the creatures of the night, but rather as a walking stick. At times, I would have to stop, for I had not prepared myself for this long a journey. My case that I had jauntily decided to take with me, weighed quite heavily and I had to adjust the heavy strap many times.

During these periods of waiting, I heard the soft breaking of the branches along one of the hedges to the road.

"Who goes there?" I cried out in French.

No response did I hear.

"I am armed!" I shouted, brandishing my makeshift club at the hedges.

I waited for quite some time in that position, fearful that perhaps my unknown assailants had not heard me, or, worse, ignored my threats.

Nothing stirred and after a while my ears became accustomed again to the night noises that are so prevalent along this road. I have to admit I felt quite foolish there having stood with my stick in the air, shouting hoarily at could only be the machinations of an over-eager imagination, one fueled by rustic French stories of wolves that could be were-wolves.

Shouldering my pack I continued down along the path. At times I had to steady myself for the path itself was, while straight, quite fraught with unfilled potholes. The shrubs loomed much closer as the fields, too, were left behind, until all that was ahead of me was simply dark and forbidding thickets from which the occasional shadow of a tree would darken my path.

At first I thought it was a night creature that had perhaps become agitated by my near proximity to its realm. But as I continued I became increasingly aware that there was something following me.

I could feel its presence near me. Occasionally it would make a noise as it pressed its way through the undergrowth. At those times I would stop and look around me, my cudgel raised, but it never did show itself at that point. I continued to be wary and look around me.

I was in such a distracted state that I was unaware of the poor repair of the road. I lurched and fell on the ground, my pack striking me with its odd angles. There I was on the ground, when something dark fleeted across the thicket in front of me. It was as large as a man with wide haunches and a lumbering gait. Its eyes flickered towards me, strange, penetrating golden slitted orbs, before disappearing back into the darkness.

I clambered up on my feet, my foot aching in protest as I gingerly put my weight on it. The night air that seemed so crisp moments before turned clammy against my skin. I scrambled for my stick that was but a dark shape against the road and had clattered far from me. I could hear the thing padding along in the brush, seeming to weave in and among the bushes.

There was a fright about me for the sound of the creature had masked itself in the many night noises and I knew for a certainty that it had followed me since Vienne. The creature kept coming closer; its breath obvious behind the thickets.

My foot protested for but a moment as I fled off the road, catching a glimpse of the creature for its great hairy bulk came into the view of the moon. And then it was hidden away by the brush as I ran through the thicket ahead of me.

Horror

I ran frightened through the thicket, branches clawing at my clothes, lashing out at my face. I could hear the crackle of the thicket behind me as the creature seemed to rush ever closer. Just when I thought this would be my end, the thickets ended in a clearing of stones; an ancient stone fence loomed across from it. The cairn stood white across a landscape of weaving claw-like shadows. I ran not heeding my own safety, perhaps in a distant part of my mind I thought that possibly a heathen circle would in some way protect me from my aggressor, or that it would slow it down enough that I could cross the fence to safety.

The monster crashed through the thicket, and within a few leaps it was upon me as it slammed into my back, the white stones on the ground coming dangerously crashing towards me. My lungs exploded from the impact, I desperately scrambled for some purchase as the creature ripped at my back. A large stone came to my hand as I twisted to look up at the creature for the first time.

It had eyes like a wolf, white, sharp teeth. The wind whipped through the thicket, rattling sharp branches against themselves, cheering on the beast. It gripped me in its talons, dragging me up to an open mouth. It looked at me with an evil cunning; with hellborne intelligence. I suspected it wanted me to scream as it salivated for my flesh, an opening course to an after theatre dinner. Instead I bashed the rock in my hand hard against its head. The strike was not Herculean, but I wounded it just the same – it howled as it flung me across the cairn with a thud, my case cracking and spilling against the rocks. I took off the case, flinging it at the dark shadow that was spreading across the rocky white face towards me.

I clamored across the white stones as they clattered angrily against me, my feet bleeding from the sharp edges. The wall was in my grasp when the creature nearly had me. Climbing over it, I was at a narrow crossroads, on one side did it end in hedges and in another was there a bit of ancient wall and a metal gate.

I flattened myself against the wall as the creature leapt over it. I gasped for a moment before scrambling towards the metal gate. Its paws thundered across the road towards me. I grasped the gate, praying to the All-Merciful Father in Heaven, feeling years of rust aching against my straining physique. It groaned enough that I was able to slip inside.

Sharing the gloom with me was an effigy of Christ our Savior, and a smaller statue dedicated to Saint Christopher, the patron saint of travelers and sailors. I hid, placing my back against the cool darkness of the back of the shrine. The creature thundered toward me and against the gate, smashing into it with its full weight, snapping what was once open now to become closed. It glanced through the bars at me with luminous eyes and snarled, spittle coming from its mouth. It grabbed the gate with its mouth and rattled it, but it stood still against his trespasses.

I prayed for deliverance as the whole shrine seemed to shake from his anger, his prize only a mere few feet away from him. Finally, it let go of the gate, glaring long and hard at me with fierce eyes. It was not an animal look, it was more that of a murderer who had decided that here was a marked man that could not be reached because of divine providence, but like the devil it was, it would soon have me in its clutches. It gripped the gate once more, but then stopped, looking past me. It hesitated, as if transfixed for but the moment, and let go. Then it left me, alone with the night and the moon.

That is how the peasants found me, curled up in the shrine, covered in blood. I was taken to safety, laid out on the farm table as a priest was sent for. All the while the peasants would mutter among themselves, but would not talk directly to me, eying me with great suspicion. I could make scarce understanding of their patois, except here seemed to be an argument of sorts going on with the owner of the farm and the growing mass outside. From what I gathered they were arguing over whether I was the fiend itself!

Before they could decide on my execution, the very kind Monsieur C. Lermarchant arrived. He turned on the people who seemed so brave moments before and made them take me to his house where his serving woman dressed my wounds and carefully listened to my tale.

It would take two days before I was well enough to rejoin my family. During this time I thought about the queer situation that I had become drawn into on that one fateful night and the only conclusion that I could draw was that it was the power of Christ who was able to deliver me from what could have been certain death, and that if I had not been so firm in my faith I would have surely perished. However, while we were waiting to depart across the channel back to England, I was approached by a rural priest who had heard my tale and had sought me out. He explained to me, in very hushed tones, that it was the statue of Saint Christopher that had saved me, that the saint himself had been born a Cynocephali, a dog-head, a were-wolf named Ruberus, and that his conversion to Christianity appeased his once bestial nature. The statue dedicated to him thwarted the beast, and thus I was left further unscathed, for exact reasons untold. I am now filled with a need to scholarly pursue some answers to this priest's allegations, and of the ordeal of which I survived – perhaps in the research to come I shall find enough lore and information to write yet another book, who knows, for it seems that very scant has been collected on

Horror

the subject of were-wolves. Beyond that I do not know what further can be lead from this tale, but that it is certain that we must prepare ourselves against the devil in whatever form he takes, whether were or wolf.

The End

Roy C. Booth hails from Bemidji, MN where he manages Roy's Comics & Games (est. 1992) with his wife and three sons. He is a published author, comedian, poet, journalist, essayist, optioned screenwriter, and internationally awarded playwright with nearly 60 stage plays published (Samuel French, Heuer, et al) with 800+ productions worldwide in 29 countries in ten languages. He is also known for collaborations with R Thomas Riley, Brian Keene, Eric M. Heideman, William F. Wu, Axel Kohagen, and others (along with his presence on the regional convention circuit). He is also presently an acquisitions editor for Indie Authors Press, London, UK/Santiago. Chile. See his entry on Wikipedia, his Facebook page, his various publishers' sites, and especially his Amazon Author Page (www.amazon.com/author/roycbooth) for more.

Walk A Mile

By Paul Mannering

I've walked more miles than I can count through this land of dust and despair. In 1932 the country was withering; dying on the vine in what the papers called the Great Depression. The poorest of us - right out there at the ends, furthest from the root – we suffered it most.

From Baltimore to Barstow, from Chesapeake Bay to Chattanooga, I rode the rails with all the other lost souls. We were the flotsam of the shipwreck, treading water until we drowned. Like a thousand others, I drifted. Taking work where I could find it, near starving when I couldn't.

I'd left Chicago with a mind to try my luck in New York, rumors abounded that work was to be found there and if not employment – then a ship to a new life somewhere. Desperation kept me moving south-east and I'd made it as far as Indiana when the soles of my boots started flapping like the panting mouth of a hound dog. The string I gagged them with had worn through again. I hurried on as the wind came down from the north and up from the south and together they stirred up those towering black clouds that smell like fresh sweat and more'n not birth a twister.

The rain came first, each drop warm like a gob of spit, and I've had my share of spitballs honked in my direction.

To begin with, the rain was almost pleasant. I tilted my face up to the deluge and washed the dust and filth of days on the road from my skin. The flush soon cooled and then I was just wet, with no shelter, and half-drowned. The only light in the afternoon sky was the lightning, cracking the firmament to shine the light of Heaven in all its glory through from the other side. At least that's what a drunken lay-preacher told me one time when we sat in a freight car on a siding outside Albuquerque during a similar storm.

Horror

My first sight of the house gave it the appearance of a picture. The lightning caught the scene in a flash like a photographer's burning bulb, rendering it in tones of bones and shadows. With all else I saw, that's the memory I have of the Durstan farm.

There were no candles or lamps flickering inside. I figured it was likely abandoned, the way so many farms and homes had been, swallowed up by the banks before they too sank out of sight.

I sat on the veranda, my back against the faded paint of the clapboard wall. The gloom of the afternoon sank into the darkness of night and I shivered myself to sleep.

The nudge of a boot woke me just after dawn. I squinted up into the glare of daylight. The shotgun in my face was no cause for alarm; I'd been warned away with worse. The woman holding the gun wore the black of a bride in mourning and her face would have been beautiful if she'd smiled.

"You need to be on your way," she said and I nodded. The seeping cold in my ragged clothes had bound itself to my skin and felt like it might be soaking into the bone.

"Yes, ma'am," I said through chattering teeth. Walking in the early morning sun would warm me up and there might be some place I could beg food further down the road.

She stepped back, her grip on the gun still firm as I climbed to my feet. The sole of my left boot stayed behind on the veranda, having come adrift in the night.

We both stared at it, myself with a strange sense of embarrassment, like I'd used her veranda as a privy and the worn and curled boot-sole was my leavings.

"You'll need some new shoes," she said.

"Yes, ma'm," I replied. There being nothing else to say.

"Stand here. Don't you leave my porch now, y'here?"

"Yes, ma'am." I'd learned that's what folks expect you to say. Nothing more than a "yessir, nosir, or ma'am." Some of the old folks I'd picked oranges or cotton, or dug ditches with, they remembered doing this kinda work, but not getting paid for it. There weren't a lot of difference between "ma'am" and "massa." Coming from someone like me, they meant the same damn thing.

I stood shivering on that porch for a long while. Desperate to take a leak, but afraid to move out to the storm-battered rose bushes or worse, have her come back before I'd buttoned up.

When she returned, she carried a bundle of clothes with a pair of shined boots on top. I blinked; the only time I saw clothes like that, they were on someone else. Someone whom, with breakfast still warm in his belly, was already thinking about what to have for lunch.

"These are my husband's clothes. The Good Book tells us to be charitable, so in the Lord's eyes it's an accounting."

I nodded, mumbling my thanks. I took the bundle, smelling the lingering scent of laundry soap and starch on the white-shirt's collar. She turned on her heel and went back inside. I stripped off my coat and shirt, pulling on the soft new fabric before she could change her mind.

Her husband was a tall man like myself, and we both had wide feet that make a pair of comfortable fitting boots a rare pleasure.

I was lacing them up good and tight when she came back, a flour sack in her hand with the smell of warm biscuits floating around it like flies circling fresh pie.

"A little food to see you down the road," she said, holding the bag out at arm's length. The shotgun had retired indoors for now.

"Thank you ma'am, much obliged." I took the bag, willing myself to wait until I was walking down the road in my new boots and clothes before I opened that sack and stuffed my wailing belly with whatever she had provided. Ducking my head in a bowing motion and trying to make myself small and less threatening, I stepped carefully off the porch. She watched me go and I could feel her unsmiling eyes boring into the back of my head even as I reached the road and kept on going. Maybe, from the back, in his clothes, I reminded her of her husband?

The flour sack had two apples and four warm biscuits in it. I ate the first biscuit without even tasting it. I slowed down and took a deep breath before starting on the second one. The smooth buttermilk taste of it was a balm to my hunger. I saved the other two biscuits; if needs be they would make a fine breakfast for the next day.

I made my bed in the dry grass under a tree that night. The sky was clear and the warmth of the day carried over past dusk. I drifted off on thoughts of warm biscuits and a house without colors. I dreamed I was walking, a common enough dream for someone who sees the same road under his feet all hours of every day. It was only when I woke up that I gave myself a grand scare. I'd never been known to sleep walk, but here I was, standing next to the rose bushes in front of the house I had left that very morning. Somehow in my somnolent state I had carried myself back here, losing a full day's travel.

I stood rooted to the spot by the shock of waking and then, without conscious command or intent, I stepped forward. My feet, still clad in the gifted boots, carried me to the steps of the dark house. I went up, a strange sense of familiarity slipping around my shoulders. I knew the grain and warp of every plank that made up this house. I had sawed and planed, shaped and nailed each length of timber, bringing a vision to life.

A house for a wife. The voice that spoke in my head wasn't mine. The name *Durstan* came to me and I knew it as well as I knew my own.

A house for a wife. There was bitterness in that phrase. As if the sweet tone of love had been corrupted by betrayal until it soured into something that would keep forever like pickled eggs in a jar.

I opened the screen door and the greased hinges barely whispered. Opening the front door, I let the screen door swing shut behind me. I left the wooden door open.

The moonlight cast a white path across the parlor and towards the kitchen. My feet turned, moving me towards what I knew was the master bedroom. I opened the next door, as the clothes I wore slid over my skin and gripped me in a fierce constriction. I felt as if I were wearing another man's hide.

She lay alone in the bed, her hair, shot with grey at the temples now, still shone like black velvet loose around her shoulders. I walked forward, right up to the edge of the wrought-iron frame. My hand reached out and gripped the heavy brass knob on the outside of the bedhead that she once told me reminded her of a fancy gate.

This was the bed we lay in, that stranger's whisper said.

My inner voice, the one that talks to me during the long hours of trudging or riding empty freight cars, began to pray. When some deep part of me felt the need to seek comfort in the divine that I had invested neither time nor trust in since I was a small child, I knew I was truly afraid.

Images came as unbidden as the rest of this waking dream. I saw a younger and fairer likeness of the woman who now lay sleeping in the bed. Then, her bare skin, pale as milk and glowing with womanly exertion, slid against my own work-worn hide in this very bed as we exulted in our love.

A house for a wife.

This memory wasn't my own. I felt a voyeur's shame and arousal as the vision swept over me and in its wake, the hair on my arms rose with the chill of a cold sense of hatred that wasn't mine either.

The iron bedstead with the brass knobs creaked under my grip. I twisted the metal sphere, feeling the thread squeal as I turned it. The woman in the bed stirred, moaning with the soft whisper of a winter wind. The heavy brass ball came off in my hand, and my arm jerked up, raising high above my head.

A house for a wife.

A house for her bones.

I saw the woman again, older now. Her unsmiling face closer to the one I had met that very morning. I wanted to scream, but the tight collar of my shirt choked me, as in my mind's eye she swung an axe, and my vision filled with red-stars.

A house for a black widow.

Whatever love had brought them together dried up and blew away with the topsoil. The drought had tanned her heart and soul, making it tough as leather and impervious to mercy.

The heavy weight crashed down like a rock.

Her eyes snapped open as the first blow struck between her eyes and broke her nose. A gurgling scream bubbled through her lips. The thick strands of drying spit stretching like spider web between her bared teeth as she cried out. The second blow of the brass knob smashed her forehead, denting the dense bone of her skull and making her eyes bulge and roll to fix on me. It was not my face she saw leaning over her and committing murder. She beheld the likeness of her dead and vengeful husband. I saw the recognition in her eyes as her sanity tore loose of its moorings.

My arm rose and fell. The soft scent of laundry soap in the cotton shirt I wore fading under the sharp stink of blood and the odor of a dying body letting loose all that it contained.

The skin of her forehead split and the bone underneath caved in like a soup bowl. My arm dropped to my side. The brass knob fell from my limp fingers and I gasped for breath. Her face had been deformed by violence and her eyes were wide and still.

The shoes on my feet turned me away from the grisly scene, walking me like a puppet until I stopped struggling and strolled meekly. I walked out of the house and into the final hour of the night.

When I reached the road I felt the grip of the suit I wore relax. My feet were my own to command again. The first thing I did was strip down to my underwear. In bare feet, shorts and sweat-soaked vest I bundled the dead man's clothes and boots up and carried them in my trembling arms. I trotted down that dusty road, with only the silver moon as a witness.

I found another farm around noon the next day. A ramshackle place, with laundry flapping in the slight breeze. I stole trousers and a shirt, figuring I could live without shoes for a day or two longer. The copper where the mistress of this shack had boiled her whites in starch still steamed over the embers of an open fire. I blew on those embers and fed the glowing grubs of fire with the dead man's clothes and boots until everything of his I had worn fell to ashes.

The End

Horror

Paul Mannering is an award winning writer living in Wellington, New Zealand, where he lives with his wife Damaris and their two cats.

Author of The Tankbread series, and Dead! Dead! Dead! published by Permuted Press.

The Drakeforth Trilogy, including book 1 "Engines of Empathy" and the forthcoming sequel, "Pisces of Fate," are published by Paper Road Press.

Paul's other writing credits include about a hundred published short stories and hours of podcast audio drama written and produced for BrokenSea Audio Productions.

Jennah

John Mc Caffrey

Calvin walked up the cracked and broken sidewalk toward the farmhouse that he once called home. The wind in the trees his only companion since Route Seven and the chatty trucker that brought him forty miles closer to Brandenville.

No street sign marked the intersection where the big rig dropped him, just as there hadn't been any when he'd first arrived in town, sixteen years before. The locals knew the dirt and gravel road off the paved two-lane as Cherry Hill Road, for it led to the cemetery of the same name. It also passed a series of the oldest farms in the area, Gram's farm being one of them. He still had a difficult time referring to the property as his. When she died, the house and land had passed to him.

You come home Calvin, you come on home soon as they let you. This is where you belong. Don't let none of those doctors tell you different boy, you belongs here.

Once on Cherry Hill Road he set off at a brisk pace, the sky, the color of cigar ash, pressing down on him as he bent into the wind. Fields bordered each side of the road, vacant and dismal due to the recent harvest. Large houses and decaying barns looked as barren as the fields they sat in, a testament to the poverty of the rural farming community Grams had lived and died in. To Calvin however, it was a welcome sight after his long hospital stay.

He let his eyes wander over Gram's farm from the front yard, the surrounding trees offering the only color as their leaves turned amber. Much of the property was as he recalled, but much also was changed, and it was due to more than just the perspective of age. He tried to recall what the house looked like before the authorities accused him of killing those two boys, taking him away when he was thirteen.

He came to live with Grams just past his tenth birthday, after an especially

Horror

bad encounter with his mother's most recent boyfriend requiring the police and nine stitches. He arrived in Brandenville with nothing more than a paper bag of old clothes and two black eyes. His last memory of his mother was her waving at the bus station between sips from a small brown bag.

You was a pitiful sight boy, all mussed up looking, like a little puppy that been whupped too many times. Lordy though, I was happy to see you. This your home now boy, no need to cry for spilt milk, this your home. This where you belong honey, this where you always belonged.

He set his suitcase down, took off his hat, and breathed in the pungent earthy scent of the farm. As he gazed at the house, youthful memories hid the decay and neglect of the passing years. He could still remember the stark-whitewashed exterior of the main house, the red shutters framing each window, with dark green wooden planter boxes under the sills. The oddly shaped weather vane that had stood proud and erect upon the tallest peak of the roof, and the wide porch that ran the entire length of the front of the house and back along the left side, ending with a swing hung from the ceiling above.

He tucked the hat into his pocket and took his gloves off, bending down to run his hands over the cold ground. He needed to feel the very dirt, as if the physical contact could dispel any doubts that might arise to convince him it wasn't real. He reached out further, touching the overgrown lawn that was now mostly weeds, drawing a deep, shuddering breath.

He was home.

His home.

This your home now, boy.

He brushed the soil from his hands as he stood, wiping at his eyes as he surveyed the front yard. Movement to his left made him turn – a darker shadow amongst the trees seemed to fade deeper into the forest. He took a step towards the woods before stopping. It was probably a deer and nothing more. She couldn't know he was home yet and even if so, she wasn't fond of the light.

"Jennah," he whispered to the trees. Even as overcast as it was, he doubted she would brave the daylight.

I think it's mighty fine you got a little friend Calvin, mighty fine. I wish I could see them too, I wish I could see your granddaddy. I miss him so. Maybe when I fade I will be with him and then you can bring us both back with that gift you got. He would sure love you Calvin. He loved your mama but he always wanted a boy.

Jennah had come to him his first summer here. Grams had indulged him, allowing him to stay up much later than was right for a ten year old, and for Calvin, the open space of the farm was the most amazing thing he'd ever seen. There were fields to run through, a forest to hide in, streams to hunt for frogs in, as well as a barn to jump out of into piles of hay below. Cows and chickens, horses, and even a goat lived on Gram's farm. For a young boy who had only known the city – and the seedier parts of it at that – it was like living within a dream.

He'd found the cemetery after being on the farm less than a month and it immediately became his favorite place. He would lie upon the weed choked grass and stare into the night sky, enjoying the solitude. The headstones marked their respective graves like granite soldiers standing at attention, his only companions.

Cherry Hill is the oldest thing in these parts Calvin. Older than the town. I went there many nights after your granddaddy died. I could hear the Twilight Folk talking to me there. I could hear them plain as day. Cherry Hill is a special place Calvin. You don't never be scared of that place, 'cuz them folks don't mean us harm, Lord no.

Cherry Hill was surrounded on three sides by forest, the open side to the old gravel road. No one went there other than a monthly state truck that brought a tractor to cut the grass. It had been designated a historical site, though no one knew anyone that was buried there, the latest tombstone dated eighteen seventy-four. Calvin found the place mysterious and wonderful, and would spend hours amongst the graves staring at the names and dates, wondering who the people had been. He was in the graveyard looking up at the stars late one evening when Jennah first appeared.

She glided over the ground silently, making her way through the granite obstacles. Blonde, shoulder length hair stirred in the warm breeze, blowing about her pale face. She was clothed in a dated denim dress and dark colored blouse, but what caught and held Calvin's attention were her eyes.

Even in the fading light, the depth and intensity of her eyes was apparent. Like twin panes of colored glass they seemed to hold a luminescence that shone from within. Although startled, he hadn't been afraid. Her sudden appearance seemed of no more consequence than a cloud passing over the moon. She walked closer, her mouth slightly open, her skin alabaster, shining like one of the Angelic statues that stood close by. She stopped a few feet from where he lay, cocking her head to one side, gazing at him.

"Hi," he said, finally finding his voice in the gloom.

She didn't respond, simply continued to hold his gaze.

"I didn't know anyone else lived close by," he went on with his one sided conversation. Although he had no experience with girls, he knew this one was pretty.

"My name is Calvin, what's yours?"

Still the pale girl didn't respond, although she stopped staring at him to regard

Horror

the night sky.

Calvin followed her gaze as she tilted her head back.

"Jennah."

Her voice was as soft and whispery as fine linen pulled across a coverlet. He was never quite sure if she had spoken aloud, or if the name had sounded in his mind. She held out her hand, leading him out of the graveyard and together they ran through the woods.

They spent that summer together, and she showed him the countryside, taking him deeper into the forest than he had ever gone alone. He would occasionally see others like her in the woods, or down by the cemetery. Though they didn't frighten him, an aura of sadness and danger hung over them, making him keep his distance. Some of them would wander by the backyard at night to speak with Gram. She enjoyed having guests again after being alone for so long.

Just 'cuz you here boy, them folks all can come around the house and keeps me company, Lord yes. When I was here alone, hardly any were ever able to come around. The gift is weak in me. Ever since you came, I can hear all kinds of them. You're able to bring more around than your mama or your great-granddaddy ever could.

He would light a candle on the evenings he could go out and place it in his bedroom window. It was a signal they'd worked out so she would know when to come meet him. It was only when his homework was done and Grams had checked it for mistakes that she would let him stay out late.

I know you took a shine to that friend of yours boy, but them townies still want you to learn your schooling. I sure don't want that fat pig of a sher'ff up here again stinking up the house asking me why I didn't put you in school in the first place, Lord no. You finish up them books then you can go out and play with your friend.

A roll of thunder in the distance interrupted the reminiscence of his childhood as the sky announced its intentions for the evening. He glanced towards the darkening heavens – nightfall was approaching.

He picked up his bag, walking the rest of the way up the sidewalk to the porch stairs. Pigeon droppings stained the surface and the paint that was visible beneath was cracked and peeling. He dug the key out of his pants pocket, inserting it into the lock. He turned it expecting resistance from age, but the key turned easily.

A small, balding man who had presented himself as Gram's attorney delivered the key to him four years ago in the hospital. He had been short and to the point, explaining to Calvin that there was an account set up to pay the taxes on the farm so that it wouldn't be a concern for him for some time. When the man left, Calvin had the key and a bank account left to him by Grams. The doctors hadn't allowed him to attend the funeral.

One day I won't be around no more Calvin. One day I'm gonna cross over. When I do, this ol' farm gonna be yours. Your mama too far gone in the head and I can't rightly trust her to do the right thing. Don't know where she is now anyway. You the only family I got.

He cocked his head to one side, listening as a strong breeze blew through the large oak in the yard, the branches swaying to the gust and making a soft sighing sound. Thunder boomed again, nearer now, the sound echoing like boulders rolling down a mountain. The porch swing swayed lazily in the breeze, chain squeaking, sounding much as he remembered so many years before.

He closed his eyes, listening to the sounds he'd missed for so long. Sounds he thought he could never forget, but time, age, and the persuasive rhetoric of the many doctors, dulled its memory in his mind. He gazed at the old porch and could almost see the paint return to its original color. The wicker chairs with their flowered cushions returned to their former luster – chairs he had sat in while the aroma of Gram's freshly baked sweets filled the air with their inviting scents.

Calvin! You come in here and get you a slice of this pie. You make sure you wash them hands of yours first. Little boys can make a mess o' themselves even when they sleeping, Lord knows.

Calvin!

He let out a loud exhale, raising a hand to his eyes. The memories of his childhood made him realize how much time had been lost while he'd been in the hospital. He stood quietly on the porch, letting his emotions wash over him. Tears of loss for the time robbed from him, tears of anger for the way the people of the town had treated him as well as sadness for being taken from the only people who ever loved him, Grams and Jennah.

He'd been waiting for this day for twelve years. Twelve years of doctors and pills, barred windows, and counselors trying to convince him that everything he told them wasn't real. That it was all a figment of his imagination, brought on by the delusions of his grandmother. That there were no Twilight Folk and there was no one called Jennah, and never had been.

The authorities concluded it was he who murdered those two boys, and that Grams lied to protect him. The police questioned them both and when Calvin related his story to them, he found himself in court where no one was really interested in anything else he had to say. The parents of both boys appeared at his hearing and their outbursts had them finally removed, but not before one of the fathers threatened Calvin in the courtroom. He looked at the man, neither in fear nor regret, for he hadn't killed his son, or the other boy for that matter. Jennah had.

Lawyers! Ha! What them people know? They know a lot of nothing boy, let them go

Horror

on and think what they want. The townies know Calvin, they don't want to admit they know, but they know. They known since my daddy first went into Cherry Hill and called to the Twilight Folks and woke them up. They been knowing ever since.

The trial proceeded, the lawyers and doctors did what was in his best interest, taking him from his grandmother to place him in the sanitarium. The doctors insisting the only way he would ever get better is if he spoke about that day in the woods.

"Calvin, there is no such person as Jennah, you must understand that she doesn't exist," Doctor Edmund said from behind his thick glasses.

"If she doesn't exist, then why do I remember her?"

"I don't know Calvin, why do you think you remember her?"

"I remember talking to you yesterday, maybe you don't exist either."

They explained to him that an extensive search of the property as well as the surrounding area had been conducted for the people he claimed lived there. They hadn't found anyone. Furthermore, they told him, they found nothing to suggest that anyone had ever lived there.

Them people from town never did take a liking to our family boy. Your mother could see the Twilight Folk somewhat, just as my daddy could. Made your mama crazy though, and sent her to the bottle when she got older. I never could see them but I sure could hear them when they come to call. You now – you just like my daddy was, but the gift be even stronger in you Calvin. You can see them can't you boy? Lord yes. I can see it in your eyes, I can feel it in you Calvin. You can call to them just the same as he could. You can call them and wake them all up if you want.

He dried his eyes on the sleeve of his jacket, picked up his bag and went inside, closing the door behind him.

Most of the furniture was missing, the few pieces that remained looked as if they were little more than home to field mice. Neighborhood kids must frequent the house, as there was a trash bag with empty beer cans in the middle of the living room. The smell of must and mildew filled the room as he stepped past the trash bag, but nothing could dampen his feeling of being home, of belonging.

The breeze blew in from the outside, down the long hallway from the kitchen into the living room, whistling and sighing. He would need to check and see how many windows were broken. He walked down the hall towards the kitchen, noticing the graffiti that had been spray painted on the walls. A boy professed his love for a girl named Sandy in red spray paint, and someone else's desire to do something sadistic and sexual to them both painted in white underneath.

He added paint to the mental list he was making for the hardware store.

He stepped into the kitchen in time to see the back door close with a click.

He stood still for a moment, listening for any sound from the back porch, but all he heard was the wind. He crossed the cracked and peeling linoleum to the window that looked out to the backyard and barn beyond.

Nothing.

Them Twilight Folk are funny Calvin. They sure don't care for the light of day, but they attracted to you like moths to a light bulb. They will come to you. You can call them without even trying.

The wind continued blowing through the house; it was possible that it might have closed the door.

It was possible.

He gazed out the window, letting his eyes play over the old barn, and as with the house, his memories masked the decay. He'd spent many nights in the loft with Jennah those first two summers, playing hide and seek or just sitting and passing the time away. He turned from the window, looking around the kitchen, again feeling the pang of nostalgia wash over him. This had been Gram's favorite room and he could almost feel her presence.

He crossed the kitchen to the table and chairs that still occupied the same spot they had many years before. The table was filthy and only one chair looked sound enough to sit in, but it was the same kitchen set that he remembered. He placed his bag on the table, pulling the chair out to sit.

The sound of tires on gravel from the front of the house stopped him and he hurried down the hall to the living room, peering out the window at the large police car in the driveway.

You be careful around that old fat man Calvin. The light of goodness does not shine in his heart. Lord no. He is wicked boy, and would like nothing more than to see harm come to you.

Sheriff Thompson, the same cop that had taken him away so many years before, was exiting the car looking intently at the house. He spotted Calvin looking at him through the window and motioned for him to come outside as he leaned back against the hood of his cruiser.

Calvin made his way out the front door and stood on the porch looking down at the Sheriff as the older man took off his hat, his eyes hidden behind dark sunglasses. He appeared to be the same as when Calvin had last seen him, pot-bellied and tall, hair steel gray and military short. His long thin features evil looking, as if anger had long ago made its home on his face and never left. His brown uniform pressed with pleats so sharp they looked as if they would cut you if you got too close.

Calvin walked out to the edge of the porch and leaned against one of the

Horror

railings. He was wary of the Sheriff, recalling all too well the last time he encountered the older man.

"Hospital called my office to inform us you'd been released," the Sheriff said as he placed his hat back on his head. "I'll be damned if I will ever understand doctors."

Calvin nodded slowly, his eyes glued to the older man.

"Get down here boy," the Sheriff pointed with his gloved hand to a spot just in front of where he stood. His lips were curled back from yellowed teeth, giving him a predatory look. The hostility emanated off him like heat from a furnace.

Calvin placed his hands in his pockets as he stepped off the porch, walking down the steps towards him. He neither hurried, nor walked slowly. His eyes never leaving the Sheriff's face as he approached.

When he stood just outside of arm's reach, Calvin stopped, gazing intently at the man before him. Now that he was closer he could see the Sheriff had in fact changed since they last saw one another. Up close he looked older, the years having carved away the ruddy complexion he recalled him having, leaving him sallow and wan. Calvin could also see he wasn't just angry, he was scared. Scared as hell.

"I don't know why them sum-bitches would ever let a murdering freak like you out, but I tell you now boy, you ain't welcome here. No sir. This ain't your town, never was. You got that?"

Calvin nodded. He wasn't the least bit upset by what the older man was telling him. He'd expected something like this from the moment he walked out of the hospital, but he was surprised that it had come about this fast.

"Reckon craziness runs in your family, don't it boy?"

Calvin remained silent, his eyes fixed on the Sheriff's sunglasses. He pushed himself off the hood of his car, pointing a finger at Calvin as he spoke. His finger stabbing the air in front of him accentuating his speech.

"You look here boy. If you know what's good for you, you will clear out of these parts as fast as you can. Accidents have a way of happening to freaks like you. You hear what I'm saying?"

Calvin nodded again, keeping any look of insolence off his face. He knew this man hated him and blamed him for what happened. He also knew that if he provoked him, it would be his word against the Sheriff's – and he knew where that would land him.

"I knew the families of both them boys, they were good people. What you did to those families just ain't right. Maybe them boys picked on you some in school but they didn't deserve to be murdered. They weren't no bastard of a drunk whore. Them families went to church every Sunday."

At the mention of his mother, Calvin's eyes narrowed. A leering smile came to the Sheriff's face as he went on speaking.

"Oh yeah, we know all about that mother of yours. She was well known in these parts after what she done. Reckon you follow in her footsteps don't you boy? Reckon the both of you just as crazy as that old bitch that owned this dump. It didn't surprise anyone when your mama left town to birth her bastard son."

Calvin stared at the older man as he spoke, but he wasn't listening anymore. He was watching the tic the Sheriff had in his upper lip as he spoke. It was as if something were just under the skin, wanting to escape. Calvin could feel the older man's nervousness and fear despite his attempt to hold himself as if he were in control. He sensed the Sheriff still didn't know how much of what Calvin had told him so many years ago was true.

He raised his eyes to look to the Sheriff's sunglasses. The older man had stopped speaking and seemed to want an answer, though he had no idea what the question had been.

"Do you hear me talking to you boy?"

"Yes sir," Calvin said.

He glared at Calvin as if he would like to snatch him where he stood and shake him like a terrier shakes a rat. His plump body was almost twitching with the pent up emotions that warred within him. Anger, fear, and resentment all shared a moment on the brow of the Sheriff. He stepped closer and it was obvious in his body language he expected Calvin to take a step back. When Calvin didn't, he jabbed his forefinger into his chest, poking him hard just below his right shoulder.

"You stay long enough to get this old wreck of a house sold and you git. You hear me boy?"

He brought his face closer to Calvin's, the smell of coffee and stale cigarettes almost choking him.

"Something will happen to you if'n you stay here. Something bad will happen, and there ain't a damn thing I will be able to do about it. Not a damn thing." The last part delivered with a sneer, the threat not lost on Calvin.

"Have you seen Jennah, Sheriff Thompson?" Calvin asked, cocking his head to one side as if listening to a melody only he could hear.

The older man's face went limp, like a window blind's cord that's been suddenly cut, it fell in shock. He stepped back, losing his composure as if he'd been slapped. His eyes darted to the woods over Calvin's shoulder as if he expected someone

Horror

to be standing there. As if he expected *her* to be standing there.

Them people in town know all about the Twilight Folk Calvin. They don't understand what they is, or the gift our family has, and they sure 'nuff don't understand what them Twilight Folks can do if 'n they get angry. But they known about them since my daddy bought this farm way back before most of these townies were here. Daddy was like you boy, the gift was strong in him and them Twilight Folk could walk and talk and do things for him. The gift wasn't as strong in me, I could only hear them, couldn't rightly ever see one. But the townies, they know they real Calvin, but they don't want them to be real. You get me boy? They don't like to know that you can see them like your great-granddaddy and your mama could. They don't like to know that you can wake them up. They remember what happened to that boy that did your mama wrong. You take care who you tell you can see them too boy.

"I think she will be coming to see me soon. In fact, I know she will. Did you know she told me that Sheriff? She told me that before you all took me away. You want to be careful with your threats Sheriff. You want to be real careful."

He backed away from Calvin, fear winning the battle of emotions on his face. His eyes scanned the woods as he turned to the right, hand close to his holster as he moved towards his cruiser. His well shined low quarters kicking the gravel as he hurried to leave. He opened the door, turning once more to face Calvin.

"You git boy. You clear out as soon as you can or you'll regret it."

With a last glance at the woods, he quickly got inside the cruiser, reversing back the way he came, microphone held to his mouth as the tires spewed gravel and dust until the car made the road. He stayed at the end of the driveway for a few moments, Calvin unable to see what he was doing due to the distance. The Sheriff finally put the car in gear, speeding off in a cloud of dust. The roar of the engine carrying back to Calvin long after the cruiser disappeared beyond the trees surrounding the farm.

He stared at the plume of dust left behind until the wind took it and blew it over the fields. The Sheriff still feared Jennah and her kin. He still feared them, although he refused to acknowledge their existence.

The whole town feared them.

He walked into the living room closing the door behind him, the darkness in the house nearly complete as the sun set further. He made his way to the kitchen until he stood once again in front of the window that looked out on the back of the property, gazing to the woods beyond. He missed the forest – the trees were old and held secrets of their own. Jennah, as did all the Twilight Folk, seemed to be in tune with the woods in a way that was uncanny. She knew when those boys had come looking for him that night, catching him behind the barn as he finished his chores. She had known what they did to him when she came to him later that evening. She had kissed his bruises and held him close as he wept tears of shame, clinging to her tightly.

My daddy tol' me that those folks knows the forest Calvin, they knows it and can feel it. They live there with it and it's a part of them as sure as your feet are a part of you. My daddy lives there now with them, and one day I will lives there too. All them folks feel life again when you around just as they did when your mama lived here. I hear them now more than I ever did before Calvin. You got the gift powerful boy, Lord yes.

Within days he forgot about the pounding he'd received from the two, in the way that boys do when they are used to being beaten by their mother's boyfriends. It was little more than a series of humiliations that for him, had become commonplace. Jennah, however, did not forget. She knew the boys would come back to hurt Calvin again, and when they did, she was waiting.

You go ahead and tell them anything you want boy, they didn't believe your mama when they came a calling after what happened to that boy that wronged her when she was young and I reckon they ain't gonna believe you neither. Let them think whatever they want, cuz it don't matter a lick what they think.

Jennah been by the house, I hear her outside and I know she be a waiting for you when you get home boy. So you go ahead on and tell them anything they want to hear. Lordy, I be a laughing here at home just thinking about the look on them people's faces when you do.

Calvin stood at the window until the darkness on the farm was absolute, lost in his thoughts. He heard a car as it raced by the front of the house, engine roaring and what sounded like kids shouting out their window. Calvin heard glass breaking and knew a bottle had been thrown at the house as they passed. The engine receded in the distance, the townies were aware that he was home.

The temperature dropped noticeably in the house, but he barely felt it as he gazed into the darkness outside – they were already approaching. He felt them more than saw them, their essence drawn to his presence. Their forms, fleeting and ephemeral as they waited for him to call them into being. The wind picked up as the rain began to fall, the drumming on the roof falling softly as the deep resonance of thunder rumbled overhead. He closed his eyes, humming a tune that had been one of Gram's favorites. The wind whistled through the house as if trying to accompany his melody.

"I'm home Grams," he whispered to the gloom.

Horror

I know you is honey, we been waiting for you. We all been waiting for you, Jennah most of all. You go on now, you call us home and we set things to right, starting with that Sheriff.

"I've missed you both."

He walked to the table where he'd left his bag. Opening it, he rummaged through the contents until he located the candle and butane lighter he'd bought at the small store after he left the hospital. He stepped to the window, placing the candle on the sill. He felt with his hand to see if the wind would extinguish the flame, then lit the wick. The soft glow of the candle pushed back the shadows of the kitchen, but he wasn't concerned with the darkness.

"I'm home," he whispered again.

As if in answer, the door to the barn slammed shut as a stronger gust of wind pushed against the window. The downpour intensified as Calvin pulled the chair from under the table to sit, as the flame from the candle pulsed and waned. The Twilight Folk surrounded the house now, their keening sighs flitting about the yard as their numbers increased, waiting for his call. Jennah was with them, as was Grams, all of them yearning for what only he could give.

The house creaked and groaned with the storm's progress, but from without, there came a hushed silence of anticipation. They waited. Jennah's voice whispered in his mind as he closed his eyes, extended his arms, and called them all home.

The End

John Mc Caffrey writes tales of horror, the supernatural, science fiction, and fantasy. Born in Illinois, he grew up on the south side of Chicago. While still in grade school, he developed a passion for reading through the works of Tolkien, Poe, and Lovecraft as well as being addicted to watching Hammer Film's at the local Saturday matinee. Today he lives in Northern Indiana with his wife where he writes in his spare time. His work has appeared in various anthologies and magazines.

His debut Novella, "Nora's Wish" is available at Amazon.com

Facebook:
www.facebook.com/pages/John-Mc-Caffrey-Authors-Page/503178623071533

jmccaffrey.com

The Shadows Draw Long

Joseph Y. Roberts

Two burro-mounted figures crested the mountain trail in quest of a fabled motherlode of gold. Charlie Hinson and Tom Sullivan of Apache Junction followed the legend to fulfill their dreams.

It was rumored that the wide valley dotted with pines and chaparral on the plateau's top into which they rode held a vast, untapped treasure. Instead, a hush covered this landscape and the shadows of the trees swallowed the sunlight. Charlie frowned, pulled a hand-drawn map from his pocket, and examined it as they rode.

Tom furrowed his brow. "Are you sure this is the place?"

"Near as I can piece from the stories, yeah."

"But you're squinting at your map. Why?"

Charlie shook his head. "It looks right, but something feels wrong. It's too quiet and no breeze is blowing. It feels... dead."

"Did the stories mention that?"

"No, and that bothers me."

"Then it bothers me too, 'cause I trust your gut feelings. You're Yaqui."

"Half," corrected Charlie.

"Same thing."

Charlie grunted.

"Where did you hear these stories?" asked Tom.

"Well..." Charlie chewed his lower lip and cast a worried gaze at Tommy, "Some from various folks in town, but most from that old Indian scout who lives just outside of town."

Tommy dropped his jaw. "Aw, Charlie. They say that fella is nuttier than squirrel shit. We're out here on his say so?"

Horror

Charlie looked down. "Um, yeah. You mad?"

Tommy held up a hand. "No, I'm not mad. Just a bit... disappointed. So you're sure what that scout told you was true?"

"Yeah, I am. His map's been right so far. I'd never steer you wrong on purpose."

"Yep, I'm your best chum. So I can tell by the look in your eyes something else is bothering you. C'mon, Charlie, out with it." Tommy flashed him a knowing smile.

"Well, he said something odd. When he told me no one ever stayed up here, I asked him if that was because it was sacred grounds. He said, 'No, far from it.' When I asked him what he meant by that, he just clammed up. He then drew this map and sent me packing. I put that out of my mind... till now."

Tommy scanned the landscape with uneasy glances. "And he said no one has prospected here? Why?"

"Don't know, Tom. But if we're the first, imagine what we could find. Even if the legends aren't true, this part of Arizona is still brimmin' with silver and gold. Our odds are good."

Tommy relaxed. "That's true. It's why my Pa brought us to Apache Junction, so he could work the mines. But you and me gotta get outta that podunk town for good. In any case, let's make camp."

They found a flat area to corral the burros. Then they picked a campsite and unpacked. By the time they were finished, the sun was setting. They heated grub and sat down beside the fire to eat.

A scratching sound whispering into their ears broke the silence of the valley. Charlie jumped and stared into the dark where the intruding noise had come.

Without pausing between bites, Tom said, "What's wrong with you?"

Charlie furrowed his brow. "I heard a sound... off in the trees."

"Yeah, so? Probably an owl or something. You act like you've never been out in the wild at night before. Sit back down and finish your hardtack."

Charlie gestured toward the brush. "There's not been a peep since we got here and then suddenly that. It doesn't make sense."

Tom didn't look up from his meal. "Maybe men aren't the only creatures who can't find their way here. Sit down, you look like an idiot."

Charlie shot Tom a wounded expression. "Don't you call me that. I deserve better from you. Remember, you trust my gut feelings?"

"You're right. Sorry. Sit down and finish your supper."

Charlie's tone was skeptical. "Well, okay, but I tell—"

Charlie jerked his head up and looked past Tommy. The scratch resounded once more, much louder this time and from a different location. The hair rose up on the back of Charlie's neck and his arms. He whispered, "Something's looking at us from over there. I feel it."

"Yeah. An owl, like I said."

Charlie shook his head. "It's not an owl. Something's not right, even with you. Why are you talking to me like that?"

Tom slammed his tin plate to the ground and barked, "Sit down, dammit."

"Alright then, I will." Charlie sat in a huff, but didn't take his eyes from that spot where the scratch came. He grumbled. "Don't blame me if something gets us while we sleep."

"I promise, Charlie, if a catamount eats us, I won't say a word."

Charlie was indignant. "I'm serious."

"So am I. Can't blame you if I'm dead, right?"

"That's nothing to joke about."

It's useless. Tommy isn't listening for some reason. That isn't like him.

Charlie picked at his food and ate in sullen silence. All the while, he could feel the weight of eyes watching them. As to the source of that gaze, Charlie could find no clue. He saw nothing odd in the blackness.

The next day, the young men explored their surroundings. Tommy used the knowledge taught to him by his father to find a likely place to start digging. Charlie, however, was looking for clues as to what had made the sounds they'd heard in the night. The search came up empty.

Tommy had better luck. He found a spot of dried clay that seemed to be part of the remains of a long dry stream. He felt if there were gold flakes or nuggets, they would likely have been deposited here. They fetched their picks and dug.

After a few hours, they found gold flakes. Tommy cut loose a rebel yell of triumph. Charlie gave a wide grin.

Charlie's grin vanished when he heard a sound nearby. His eyes darted toward its direction. "Something growled. Over there."

"Not this horseshit again. You just heard the echo of my yell, that's all."

"There's something out there. We're not alone."

Tommy threw his pick to the ground and grabbed Charlie's left arm. "You're starting to piss me off."

Much to Charlie's own surprise, he threw a right cross to Tommy's jaw and knocked him to the ground. Tommy sat up, rubbed his chin, and stared at Charlie in shock. Charlie glanced at his right hand in puzzlement.

My fist did that on its own. How?

Horror

"You shouldn't grab me like that. Are you alright?"

Tom spat blood and felt inside his mouth with a finger. "I still have all my teeth and my jaw ain't busted, so I guess so. Hell, I didn't know you could hit like that. What's got into you?"

Charlie dropped to his knees beside his friend. His face was lined with guilt. "I'm powerful sorry, Tommy. I didn't mean to hurt you."

"No, don't say you're sorry. I had it coming. It's just you've always been a peaceful guy. Not like you to throw a punch. Come on, let's dig a bit deeper. Then let's call it a day."

"Well, okay. But, Tommy, you gotta start listening to me again."

They helped each other to their feet.

Tom nodded. "I'll think about it. Okay?"

Charlie frowned. "Alright... I guess."

That night, there was no return of the scratching. Weary from the long day of hard work, the young men readied their bedrolls right after eating.

They froze when they heard a sound like a choir jabbering incomprehensible chants backed by hundreds of steel tools being sharpened on grinding wheels. They heard terrified braying.

"Something's after the burros!" cried Tommy.

They snatched up their cast iron cookware and ran off to the rope corral. They found the burros pushing against the rope on one side of the corral, their eyes wild with fear. The strange sound came from the chaparral at the opposite end. Charlie and Tommy ducked under the rope, stood at the center of the corral between the burros and the sound. They shouted and banged the cookware to make a raucous din. The sound stopped and the burros calmed down. The men strained their eyes to see what lurked in the bushes.

"Could you see anything out there?" asked Tom.

Charlie shook his head. "Nope. Just that noise."

"What the hell was that sound?"

"No clue. But whatever it was, the burros knew it was bad."

Tommy rubbed the back of his neck. "Okay. From now on, we wear our guns."

"You'll get no argument out of me."

The next morning, they trudged back out to the work site, pistol holsters slung on their belts. When they arrived, they gawked in confusion.

"What the hell?" shouted Tommy.

The pit they had dug throughout the prior day was refilled with the dirt

displaced from it. Their picks had been thrown into the nearby trees, caught in the branches high above their heads.

"No animal did this, Tommy. I told you we weren't alone."

Tom's face was red with fury. He pulled his pistol and fired a round into the air. "Whoever you are out there, know we're armed and we won't hesitate to shoot. So if you wanna die, just keep screwing with us!" he shouted to the sky, his voice echoing off the far valley walls.

"I've never seen you like this."

"You've never seen me pushed this far," Tom said as he re-holstered his gun.

"So what do we do now?"

"Knock those picks out of the branches with rocks and start digging again. We know there's gold here."

As they did this, once more, Charlie could feel eyes upon them. He said nothing for the time being. He hoped, with Tommy's threat, things would settle down.

When they returned to camp, they found their fire pit covered with soil, their lanterns missing, and their bedrolls shredded into rags.

"That's two!" yelled Tommy.

"So the only light we'll have is the fire and we'll need the horse blankets to keep warm."

"Looks like," muttered Tommy.

That night, the scratching returned. Tommy fired into the dark toward the source. Every time, the noise moved and was unaffected. Tom cursed and rammed his pistol into his holster.

Tom growled. "Just a damn waste of ammo."

The next day, as they were digging their pit clear once again, Charlie stopped and leaned on his pick. "Tom, we need to talk."

Without pausing, Tom said, "No, we need to work. Keep digging."

"Okay, this is what I meant about not listening to me. I'm gonna speak whether you listen to me or not."

Tommy grumbled, put his pick down and sat on the edge of the pit. He folded his arms. "Okay. So speak."

Charlie leaned in close. "There's something unnatural about this place. We've been here for days and seen nothing bigger than a pack rat. There's been no squirrels, no jackrabbits, no sign of anything with four legs other than our burros. There's been not a single bird in the sky or in the trees. No pinyon jays, no red-tail hawks, no buzzards. That's why there's no sound. There's been no sign of

Horror

anything or anyone other than the plants and us. Yet things keep happening. Things that need hands. It's just damn weird."

Tom's eyes narrowed. "Yeah, I noticed that. Just us. So I got an idea. I think you've been doing this shit because you're sore I won't listen to you."

Charlie's jaw dropped. "What? What do I gain from that? That's just crazy, Tommy."

Tom nodded. "Oh, there's crazy alright. I think it's you." His finger poked Charlie's chest.

He swatted Tom's hand away. "How can you say that to me?"

"Easy. Like you said, there's just us and I know it's not me doing this shit. Maybe you went crazy in the heat? Maybe caught it from that Indian scout? How can I tell? I know this, we can't go on like this."

"What... are you saying, Tom?"

Tom's voice turned to a growl. "We call it quits. We divide up the gold dust and leave this damn place. When we get off the mountain, we go our separate ways."

Charlie shook his head and pleaded, "Tommy, no. We're--"

"Nothing! I'm white and you're a half-breed. A damn crazy one at that. I'm done with you, Charlie Hinson."

His face red and tears streaming from his eyes, Charlie barked, "Then you can go straight to hell, Tom Sullivan."

"After you, Breed."

The former friends stormed their way back to their camp, sorted the gold dust, and packed up the camp. They went to retrieve the burros and load them.

Arriving at the corral, they stood in slack-jawed astonishment. Charlie broke their silence. "I told you. So how the hell did I do this?"

Before them, at the middle of the rope corral, lay a bloody pile of shredded flesh with pink broken bones sticking out at random angles. Slung over the ropes were a pair of brown hides. Blood stained the ground in all directions.

Tommy's reply was soft and sheepish. "You couldn't have. You've never been out of my sight. Maybe it was a catamount."

Charlie pointed. "There's no paw prints in the dirt. Besides, no catamount kill ever looked like this. So what do we do now?"

Tom shook his head and rubbed his face. "I don't know. We're stuck here."

"Let's get back to camp before something else happens. We can't do anything here."

At camp, they sat in stunned silence. Many hours passed as they struggled to understand how the impossible had happened. No answer presented itself. Charlie broke the quiet once more. "You know I'm right. There's something in this valley that no one has seen before, something no man can understand. Why won't you admit that?"

Tom scowled. "Okay, I admit it. But I don't see what we can do about it."

Charlie scratched at his black, wiry beard. "I don't either. But we haven't been ourselves for some ungodly reason. I punched you and I'd never do that. And I'm sorry I told you to go to hell. I don't want that. I consider you my blood brother."

Tom gave a slow nod. "You're right. You're usually right. I just don't give you credit. We're not nothing."

The men gave a single nod in unison.

Charlie flashed Tom a small smile. "Now we just need to figure out how to get out of here."

Tom shrugged. "I don't see any other way. Tomorrow, we start walking."

"Okay, we walk."

As the sun sank, they turned in for the night.

Charlie woke, as usual, to the rising sun in his eyes. Nothing odd had happened during the night. Charlie heaved a sigh of relief. He sat up and, looking over, saw that Tom was still sleeping, face down.

He called out. "Hey, sleepy head. Time to wake up and start walking."

Tom continued to lay still.

"Hey, Tommy. Wake up," Charlie said loud enough for his voice to echo off the valley rim.

Still Tom did not stir.

"Hey, let's get started." He strode over to Tommy's prone form. He shook him. Tom was hard to the touch. Charlie noticed a telltale tuft of reddish hair curling up from below the back of Tommy's hairline. He knew it well from working with Tom shirtless in hot weather. It was his patch of chest hair.

Below the back of his head?

Charlie pulled off the horse blanket to find Tommy's body lying in a supine position; toes up to the sky. He froze and stared unbelieving.

In his mind, panic raced and flowed.

OhmyGodTomisdeadwhokilledhimamInext?

The only sound that escaped his lips were his wails of grief and terror echoing off the valley ridges.

He collapsed onto the ground, hugged his knees and rocked back and forth. All the while, he stared at Tommy's corpse as, in his mind, time became unhinged. The sun arced overhead. As it sank toward the west, Charlie started talking to

Horror

his dead friend. "What do I do now, Tom? Why are you dead? Did I die last night and go to hell? Seems like it. Answer me."

The unnatural silence of the valley was his reply.

The golden rays of the sunset shocked Charlie to action. His heart pounded and his mouth went dry. His breath came in tight gasps of panic. Like a frightened mouse, he sought cover. He found a crevice behind a large boulder just out of sight of the camp where he could hide. He hoped his concealment would elude whatever had killed Tom. Twilight fell and night wrapped around him like a burial shroud.

An unknown period passed. Charlie snapped to full alertness when he heard the scratching sound. He held his breath. In the faint starlight, he could see shadows flowing along the ground like molten wax from a spilt candle among the Pinyons and chaparral. He heard a hissing noise above his head. Charlie slowly raised his eyes upward.

Atop the boulder next to him, an inky shape hunkered, silhouetted by the arc of the Milky Way behind it. He thought he could see bats ears rising up from what should be its head. Two large, pale, pupil-less white orbs gazed down upon him. Charlie's breath caught in his throat. His heart raced. He tried desperately to melt into the rock face.

Charlie's heart nearly seized when this shape stood, jumped down into the opening of the crevice before him and slid closer toward him. He was trapped. A small, strangled gasp slipped from his throat. His mind reeled in an effort to comprehend what his eyes were seeing. The figure moved in a disjointed way that made it seem that each part that moved had suddenly appeared from around a corner. An odd scent, like a mix of roses and cow flop, wafted into his nostrils. Charlie shrank deeper into the crack, without luck, as the thing leaned near him. It sniffed at him, seeking his scent. It drew back and started hissing. Charlie thought he could hear words in the hissing, but if so, it was a language unknown to him. He made out one word, "Saldoop." It meant nothing to him.

Through lips shuddering with fear, Charlie asked, "What are you?"

More hissing was his reward.

Charlie wanted this nightmarish shadowy specter to back away.

His desperation for distance allowed him to overcome his terror. He pulled his knife and stabbed at the thing's "chest." The blade snapped off and felt to Charlie as if he'd tried to stab a mountain.

Inky claws seized his forearms and, with a strength impossible to resist, jerked him from the crevice and hurled him through the air. Charlie struck the ground hard and his head hit a rock. His senses swam for a moment, then faded.

When Charlie came to, the sun was already at the zenith. He slowly sat up. His head pounded and an egg had swelled on his forehead. He ached everywhere and his shoulders felt as if someone had tried to pull his arms off. He looked over toward where Tommy lay and saw that the creature had been busy.

Tom's body was tied to a makeshift travois. Charlie flushed with anger when he saw Tommy had been bound like a sack of feed, with no regard to human dignity. The rope looped carelessly around his neck was particularly insulting. He knelt next to the cadaver and examined it closely. He retied the binding ropes so that Tom's neck was free.

Then he made the mistake of looking at Tom's face. His skin was pale like clay. A tiny trickle of dried blood trailed off from his mouth. His watery blue eyes were fixed in a glassy stare. The worst thing was the expression locked on his face: sheer terror. Tommy had seen his death coming and died in fear.

Charlie moved away, puked, and wept. He punched the ground. "I'm gonna make it pay for this, I swear Tommy."

Charlie noticed something had been drawn in the dirt. It was a crude picture showing a stick figure pulling another one along on a travois. It was facing toward a sun on a horizon. Charlie sneered and rubbed the drawing out with his foot.

He growled. "So you want me to haul Tommy out of here like garbage. I think I'll send you back to hell where you came from, instead."

So Charlie sat next to Tommy and checked the workings of his six-shooter. He would bide his time till it was dark. The day passed.

Charlie dozed off, but was awakened by the now-familiar scratching. He stood with his pistol at the ready. He saw the liquid shadow flow toward him from the tree line. Charlie didn't balk; he aimed and fired. Nothing happened. The shadow kept flowing. Charlie fired twice more, but still to no effect. He began to pant, his courage leaking away. Charlie pivoted around to his rear when he heard a hiss behind him.

The thing rose up before him, blacker than the night. The enormous pale globes held him transfixed. He made a small choking sound as the thing "smiled." A vast slit opened up along the bottom of its head, displaying a seemingly endless row of sharp, conical, obsidian fangs. It was clear to Charlie it could bite off his head in a single snap of those unholy jaws.

Now Charlie balked. One of the being's hands flashed out and slapped the pistol from Charlie's grip with no effort. Then the hand turned palm out and slammed into Charlie's chest. He flew backwards like a leaf in a gust of wind

Horror

and crashed to the ground on his back. The breath was knocked from him and he struggled to inhale.

Before the starry night sky above him, Charlie saw the inky shape of the creature slide into view, standing at his feet. Its great, luminous eyes regarded him coldly.

Charlie nearly gave up the effort to breathe when he saw another shape slide into view at his head. Two more pale globes gazed down at him. Then another pair. And another. By the time he caught his breath, Charlie was surrounded by what seemed like a circle of twelve pallid, full moons. Fear tightened his throat and threatened to strangle him. A tightness in his chest made it feel as if a fist was crushing his heart. Deep inside, he longed for the release of death to end this nightmare. The shape at his feet hissed at Charlie.

Charlie croaked out, "Who are you? What do you want?"

The shadow at his head reached out a sinuous finger and drew marks in the dirt as they hissed. The shapes were cryptic and said little to Charlie. But he did puzzle out symbols of a sun arc and a repeat of the figure dragging the travois. Then he noticed a spiral symbol he knew. He had seen it on rock paintings made by the Anasazi: it represented the entrance to the Underworld. Encircling the spiral were figures like the shadowy beings around him. They appeared to be guarding it. A motion of the being's hand recaptured his attention. It finished by pointing at him, then to its mouth, then snapping its jaws shut. Charlie swallowed. He knew what that meant. If he didn't leave, they would eat him.

Charlie saw their eyes grow larger. He realized they were leaning in toward him. The twelve pale moons loomed in his view, pressing down on him. He knew then how the field mouse feels as it glimpses the red-tailed hawk's talons close in on it. Charlie's heart pounded near to bursting.

No escape. No hope. I'm their prey.

He threw his arms over his eyes, gave a high, keening scream, and rolled onto his belly. He waited for the inky claws to shred him like the burros.

The next thing Charlie knew, sunlight was filling his eyes. He was still lying on his stomach and was amazed to be alive. He recalled the thing's promise of death and shot to his feet. He found his gun and holstered it. Charlie grabbed what he could comfortably carry and the travois with Tommy's body. He made tracks to the east as suggested by the dirt drawing. After a couple of hours, he crossed over the eastern ridge and left the valley. He blazed a new switch-back path down to a smaller plain below. When he could hear birds and other wildlife, he guessed he was safe.

He had dragged Tommy as far as he could. Charlie found a clear, flat area and began to dig with his hands. The soil was too hard, so he only managed to scrape a shallow dish-like depression. He placed Tommy's body in the center of this and then covered him with stones to form a cairn. This, he hoped, would protect Tommy from scavengers. On a large, flat piece of sandstone, Charlie carved Tom's name and his birth and death years with the stubby remains of his knife. After some reflection, he added this epitaph, "No man was a better friend." He placed this tombstone at the head of the cairn, then leaned on it and wept.

As Charlie put his things on the travois and made his way on to the east, he began to talk to himself.

"This will be tough going, I know it. The desert will probably kill me. But that's okay. I'd damn sight rather have a clean death at a catamount's claws or a coyote pack than by those things. But if it doesn't..." He tossed the pouch of the gold dust in his hand. Charlie became wistful. "...But if I could, I'd give this back to have Tommy alive again."

When the sun dropped to the horizon, Charlie made camp for the night in a copse of Pinyon pines. He wrapped himself in his horse blanket to sleep. Later that night, Charlie's eyes shot open, startled awake by a noise. He had heard a scratching sound off in the brush.

"Oh, god. I didn't go far enough," he gasped.

A shadow drew across the Milky Way as two pale moons arced into view.

The End

Born in suburban Los Angeles, **Joseph Y. Roberts** describes himself as "a small town boy from a big city." His interests are eclectic, like the subjects of his fiction, which reflect an ongoing fascination with the less-traveled places of the world and history. His goal is to bring the forgotten and ignored into the light with his tales, many being historic fiction with a literary spin.

His contribution to this anthology was born from his own heritage, which includes Native American ancestry, and his intrigue with the darker mythology and legends of the American Southwest. Beings hostile to humanity haunt the mesas and canyons of this land, according to its indigenous peoples.

Joseph's favorite subjects include science fiction, military and ancient history,

Horror

archeology, progressive rock, astronomy, and table-top role-playing games. His favorite bands are Hawkwind, U2, and Pink Floyd.

Among his pursuits and occupations have been college radio DJ, actor, vacation resort sketch artist, and newspaper graphic artist. He still hopes to learn horseback riding, archery, and Kendo. Like a watermelon dropped from a great height, he's all over the map.

https://www.facebook.com/joseph.y.roberts.author
http://ljhornmoy57.tumblr.com

The Mask

Jim Tritten

The eyes…the eyes…the eyes. He tried to turn away, but his muscles wouldn't obey. His head spun back to stare at…*the eyes.* Light Robin's egg blue irises not even found in most Scandinavians. A dilated pupil in the center of wide-open eyes strongly suggested visceral pleasure. The smudged whites were ravaged by age. *The eyes.* They bulged noticeably from the face. Large black lashes ringed the lids, abnormally spaced apart–frozen open in astonishment. *The eyes…the eyes…the eyes.*

"The eyes are extraordinary, aren't they?"

He turned to face the voice of a young Hispanic male dressed in a dark suit and sporting a red tie.

"Yes, I can hardly see anything else."

"Pardon me for interrupting, but I thought I might be able to help you. Permit me to introduce myself. My name is Diego Montoya. The clerk here in the gift shop called me. I have some expertise in these indigenous Mexican masks. Perhaps I might assist?"

They shook hands.

Diego continued, "I'm the assistant curator here at the *Museo Nacional de Antropología y de Arte Indígenas.*"

"Nice to meet you, Diego. I'm Renato Pérez, from New Mexico."

"Small world, I'm originally from Albuquerque and I received graduate and undergraduate degrees from the University of New Mexico."

Renato smiled. "Go Lobos."

"What are you doing here in old Mexico, Renato?"

"I thought I'd come and do a bit of genealogical research. Family folklore says we're descendants of a conquistador who accompanied Oñate. I confess I'm totally captivated by these masks. My father has a collection of historic indigenous Mexican masks. We've exhibited them throughout the southwest.

Horror

I've been thinking about starting my own collection."

Diego turned to view the wall. "Yes, these old masks can certainly captivate. Take, for example, this one. Once you can break free of the eyes…." Diego pointed at the mask. "Consider the overall shape of the face. It's Caucasian—larger than life-sized by about half, but proportionally accurate. Notice the skin, more of a pinkish hue than found in most Hispanics."

"Why would they exaggerate the skin tone?"

"Many of these theatrical masks were supposed to be a parody of the Spanish. They have purposely exaggerated features. The eyes are obviously larger than life and so is the nose." Diego explained, "Yes, the nose is hooked, further extending the overall mass. Bulbous. Look at the flared nostrils—like the nostrils when a bull is about to charge. The red paint on the inside of the nostrils makes you wonder whether the idea was to emphasize the internal blood of the character."

"Did the indigenous peoples have such hooked noses?"

"Not normally, but this is not a mask depicting a native. The mask represents a European."

"The nose is bigger and the ears are fuller than those on any person I've ever seen."

"Yes, artistic license. Exaggerations perhaps to indicate the character had excellent hearing. The ears are normally shaped. Perhaps larger than on most people. A surprisingly small lobe extension at the bottom."

Renato leaned to the left and the right to view the ears from a different perspective. "Do you know where this mask originated?"

"We do. This is an original from the *Tlaxcaltec* people."

Renato interrupted. "Say that again?"

"Of course, it is pronounced 'lash caltec.' They originated in what is now a state east of Mexico City. The ancient Tlaxcaltecs allied with Hernán Cortés and helped overthrow the Aztec Empire. They had a major role taking the capital city Tenochtitlan. Their language was Nahuatl. Can you say 'nah watl?'" Diego reached up, lifted the mask from its peg on the wall, and handed it to Renato.

Renato mumbled "nah watl" then added, "Surprisingly light."

"Yes, carved from *zompantle*, a soft white wood native to eastern Mexico. Easy to work by hand with basic tools."

Renato rotated the mask and ran his hand over the cheeks. "The finish is smooth."

"Burned to remove splinters. Then sanded and polished before being painted. Look at these eyebrows." Diego pointed to the face. "Painted on."

Renato fingered strands of long black hair hanging over the ears. "The entire mask is not wood." He ran his hand across the top and across smaller locks dangling over the forehead.

"No, most often on a mask like this, the creator used horse hair. I'm not sure about this one, though. Might be actual human hair."

Renato's stomach tightened as he took a rapid, light breath. "Human hair?"

"Yes, sometimes the masks were made to represent a specific individual and the use of original hair or teeth was considered appropriate."

"Teeth?"

Diego laughed, "Yes my friend, but not in a mask like this. Look!" He took the mask from Renato and turned it face up with the mouth clearly displayed. "The mandible on this character juts forward so the elongated, massive lower teeth clear the upper lip and appear outside the mouth."

"These two are extra long."

"Yes, the lower canines are extremely exaggerated and connected to only three lower incisors."

"What are they made from?"

"This is some carved wood added to the main portion of the mask. Real teeth were probably too difficult or simply not available."

Renato touched the large dirty white teeth and peered inside. "I can't see anything inside the mouth."

"No, the artist wanted you to focus on the power of these teeth, perhaps indicating the model had powerful jaws and could tear you apart."

Renato shuddered and felt his mouth lower into a grimace. "The lips are a bright blood red. Matches the inside of the nostrils. Also this reddish tinge around the mouth, on the cheeks. Even on the top of the hook on the nose."

Diego chuckled. "Yes, perhaps he ate something and didn't have a napkin."

"The character appears to be old. These painted lines represent wrinkles, right?"

Diego rotated the mask to expose the multiple lines streaking the cheeks, nose, and brow. "Wrinkles for sure. Sometimes the mask is made more horrible than the original character, especially if the mask was used in a pageant. For example, those used in the *Baile de los Viejitos* depict wrinkled old men. When you analyze the performance, the dance and masks simply make fun of old men for their lecherous behavior. So perhaps this character also is supposed to be mocked."

"Or feared. Why does it have these slits under the eyes? I can look right through the mask."

"Of course, how else would the wearer see?" Diego handed the mask to Renato. "Put it over your face and look in the mirror."

Horror

Renato stepped to his left and lifted the mask in front of his face. He could smell paint, varnish, and a hint of burned wood. He shook his head and fit it to the inside of the hollowed-out back of the mask. The wood was rough on his skin. The black hair hung over his scalp and tickled the back of his neck. After a minor adjustment, he could see through the slits. Renato's body tensed and breathing ceased. His skin tingled as the tickling from the back of his neck spread down his chest and up into his face. He turned and gazed into the mirror. *The eyes...the eyes...the eyes...*

Diego clasped his right shoulder. "The mask, my friend, is called *temiktiloni*, in Nahuatl."

Renato spoke through the mask, "What does that mean, Diego?"

"*El asesino*, my friend...The Killer."

"What's this?" The Dallas-Fort Worth Airport customs agent stood back, eyes wide-open, gaping at the shiny piece of wood with dark stone chips along the edges.

Renato finished the unwrapping to reveal a three-foot-long weapon. "It's called a *macuahuitl*."

The agent squinted her eyes and nose.

Renato explained, "maque awitl." Renato turned the blade to reveal the other side. "The word comes from an indigenous Mexican language known as Nahuatl."

"Is this a sword?" The agent's face screwed up as she shook it from side to side.

"No, more like a long flat ax but look here, it's shaped like a cricket bat. You pick it up by this grip—with this one you can only fit one hand around it."

Renato grasped the light green handle shaped like a snake but decided he wouldn't use it to illustrate his next point. "You'd swing it through the air." He laid the weapon back down and swung his empty hand above his head in a broad circular motion. He made a "swooshing" sound with his mouth.

"What are those teeth along the sides? Aren't they sharp?" The agent ran her forefinger along the outer edge of the dark stones. "Ouch!" Blood oozed from a long, thin wound.

"Those are obsidian shards. Notice how they are fit to both sides of this polished flat piece of wood. They're extremely sharp as you just found out."

The agent placed her finger in her mouth and nodded. "Yes."

"It's one continuous piece of wood. A strong warrior would use this weapon to decapitate a horse. Well, the taller two-handed version could. This one might easily take off a human head."

The agent's mouth turned down, and her nostrils flared. "Is the…manchuka…real?"

"*Macuahuitl.* Try it—maque awitl."

"Forget it."

"No, this is only a replica. The last known original burned in Madrid over a hundred years ago." Renato sensed he was not going to have a problem with the agent. He re-wrapped the macuahuitl, careful not to touch the razor sharp dark pieces of stone. Renato saw the agent shift her attention to the bubble wrap still in his luggage.

"What's in there?"

"A mask."

"Let's see."

Renato lifted the mask out of the bubble wrap package and set it on the examination table. He peeled back the tape holding the package together. When he took off the last layer of covering, he stepped aside to allow the agent a direct view.

The agent recoiled, eyes wide open. "Good God, those eyes are…well, the whole thing. I mean, it's disgusting. Why in the hell would you want to bring anything like that out of Mexico? Should've left it behind for the cartels. What you gonna do with it?" She shook her head as she held a tight grimace.

"Put in on the wall of my house, along with the macuahuitl."

"You crazy? I hope you don't have a wife or girlfriend. No way I'd let anyone put up those things in my house. Why don't you give it to someone you really, I mean really, hate? You got an ex who's sucking you dry?"

Renato turned his back to the agent and re-wrapped the mask. His hands trembled as they made contact with the hair.

"Reminds me of folklore tales told by my granny. You better watch out having those things around. Might be more to the story than you know. Take that ugly mask and the manchuka thing…or whatever the hell you called it…and get outta here."

Joycelyn smiled at Renato, withdrew her key from the lock to his house, and stepped through the door. "Welcome home, my dear."

Renato rushed forward to give the blonde a warm hug and a kiss. "Welcome back, yourself. How was Washington?"

"Exciting as always. Can't wait for the day I actually get a job at headquarters. This back and forth is killing me. How was the flight back from Mexico?"

Horror

"Not too bad. I wish you could've come visit me, for part of the time anyway."

"I would've if I could've swung the time off. Always another crisis. Never ends." She dropped her purse on the table near the door and her luggage on the mat. "So, what's got you so excited you wanted to show me something right away?"

"First a glass of wine." They moved to the sofa and Renato poured from the bottle he had been decanting. "*Salud.*" They clinked glasses, and sat a while as they got caught up.

"So you verified your family came with Oñate from *Santa Bárbara*, that's south of Chihuahua, right?"

"Yes, although the origins of the expedition are in the silver mining area around Zacatecas. What I found most interesting is that our family roots go back to the original conquest of the Aztec Empire by Hernán Cortés. The first Pérez must have come over on the initial expedition from Cuba."

"Not too many people I know can trace their lineage back to Cortés."

"What I really want to show you are some of the artifacts I brought back with me." Renato refilled their glasses and led Joycelyn into his study.

As she entered the room, Joycelyn's left hand flew up to her mouth as she inhaled sharply. "My God, what's that?"

"Striking, isn't it?" Renato beamed.

"The eyes, they're horrible." She lowered her hand and inched closer to the mask hanging on the wall.

"It's a theatrical prop."

Joycelyn backed away from the wall. "What possessed you to bring such a grotesque object back here?"

"I don't know. It's like I had this overwhelming need to take it." Renato walked over to the mask and touched the left cheek. "Fortunately this beauty was for sale in a museum gift shop."

"Beauty? Really? Sure they didn't pay you to take it?" She finished her wine and extended her glass for a refill.

Renato chuckled and filled both glasses. "No, but the price was quite reasonable. On the other hand, the macuahuitl was a bit expensive." He lifted the weapon off its mounting and held it out to her.

"Do they go together?" Joycelyn backed away from the macuahuitl and sat on the corner of the desk.

"No, the macuahuitl is a replica of what the ancient indigenous peoples used to fight my ancestors. The mask was used in some village pageant. Absolutely nothing to do with each other." He put the weapon back on its wall mounting underneath the mask. "I find them absolutely captivating."

"Well, I might think of a few other words to describe both of these things. Why would you want to put them where you can see them when you're working at your computer?"

"I only want to admire them for a while. Perhaps I will find another place for them at some point."

"Would you like a suggestion? Why not put them in the garage?"

Renato frowned. "You're an educated woman. Why would you let some inanimate historical items get to you?"

"Because I am getting some very bad vibes just being near them."

"Really? They're lifeless—made out of dead wood."

"Why would you want to have that ugly face staring at you? Why would you want a weapon like this in your house? I mean, if I looked at those two things every day, I'd have nightmares. Don't even think about putting them in the bedroom."

"Well, I don't plan to do anything other than to admire them when I'm at my computer."

"Renato, you need to think seriously about the effect having such negative artifacts in your home will have on you. Or us!"

"What are you talking about? These are hunks of wood. They can't affect anything."

"Renato, they have terrible vibrations. There's something odd about them, especially the mask." Joycelyn rose and stood in front of Renato, arms crossed, eyes squinting as she looked directly at him. "I'm not going to spend any more time here as long as these…things…are hanging in public. You put them away somewhere, and I'll be back. Thank God I kept my apartment." Joycelyn turned and marched out of the room.

Renato heard the front door slam, and he refilled his glass. *Women can be so….* He walked up to the wall and pondered his two new acquisitions. *Two hunks of wood.* He reached up and lifted the mask off its peg, brushing back the hair. *Can't hurt anything.*

He turned towards the mirror and held up the mask in front of his face. Renato shook his head and fit it to the inside of the hollowed-out back of the mask. He could smell paint, varnish, and a hint of burned wood. The wood was rough on his skin. The black hair hung over his scalp and tickled the back of his neck. After a minor adjustment, he could see through the slits. Renato's body tensed and his breathing ceased. His skin tingled as the tickling from the back of his neck spread down his chest and up into his face. He turned and gazed into the mirror. *The eyes…the eyes…the eyes….*

Horror

Renato sat in front of his computer. He read the text.

> "The purpose of the masks is to convert participants into other beings or characters."

This site usually has good information.

> "Jaguar and eagle warriors dressed themselves like these animals in order to gain their strengths."

Renato rose from his chair and walked over to the mask. He reached up, took the mask from its peg and put it over his face—not too close. He turned to review his image in the mirror and moved the mask to the side so he could see himself. Nothing special happened. *Must have had too much to drink last night.*

Renato shifted his view to the macuahuitl. He put the mask back on its peg and picked up the weapon, careful not to nick himself. *Heavier than the mask.* He hunkered down and raised the weapon over his head. Renato admired himself in the mirror and smiled.

After returning the weapon to its wall mounting, Renato glanced at the clock. Time to call Diego. He sat and dialed on his Skype phone +52 55....

"¡Diga!"

"Diego, *hola*, it's Renato from New Mexico."

"*Hola mi amigo*." They exchanged pleasantries for a few minutes before getting down to business.

Diego continued. "The Tlaxcaltecs who made the mask were taken from their native area and used by the Spanish to set an example for other indigenous peoples. They modeled good behavior and were used to work in the mines. The museum obtained this mask from a collector in Zacatecas."

"Zacatecas, the area where my family originated. They came north with Oñate."

"Tlaxcaltecs were involved with a series of rebellions by the native population. The Tlaxcaltecs fought on the side of the Spanish. They defeated the Zacatecos in an uprising that started after Coronado left the province to explore the north."

"So what does all this ancient history have to do with the mask?"

"The mask dates from the mid-16th Century. From what we can tell, it was used for about fifty years by the Zacatecos. By that time, some of the native groups had changed sides and were now allied with the Spanish. This specific mask was used in a type of theatrical performance teaching taboos. Might explain why the figure is a Caucasian parody."

"You told me at the museum the mask was of Tlaxcaltec origin. Any idea why the mask was made by one group and used by another? Why does it deliberately have grotesque European features if used to teach law and order? I would think a teaching mask would be stern and powerful."

"No, but maybe I can contact the collector. Wonder if he's still alive? All we know is the Zacatecos stopped using the mask around the same time as they were wiped out. It was a combination of combat and smallpox that did them in. About the time Oñate left Zacatecas for *Santa Bárbara*."

"That's strange."

"Surviving remnants of all of these groups intermarried with the Spanish and lost their own separate cultural identities. Most of the cultural possessions from groups like these were sold off to feed the survivors. The mask probably traded hands dozens of times before ending up with the collector who sold it to the museum."

"Thanks for the info, Diego. Shoot me an email if you find out anything more, and we'll talk again."

Renato clicked the keys and commanded his computer to find Zacatecos. In an instant, on his screen were images of Spanish *conquistadores* with their allied Tlaxcaltec warriors holding macuahuitls, doing battle with the rebellious Zacatecos.

Renato turned toward the mirror and held the mask in front of his face. Leaning his head forward, he loosely put it into the hollowed-out back of the mask. He could smell paint, varnish, and a hint of burned wood. He shook his head and fit it to the inside of the hollowed-out back of the mask. The wood was rough on his skin. The black hair hung over his scalp and tickled the back of his neck. After a minor adjustment, he could see through the slits. Renato's body tensed and breathing ceased. His skin tingled as the tickling from the back of his neck spread down his chest and up into his face. *The eyes…the eyes…the eyes….*

"Hello, anybody home?"

Renato ripped the mask off and hustled it inside the armoire. "In here, honey." He closed the door to the cabinet.

"I smell steaks. So what'cha doin' in here?" Joycelyn walked into the study twirling her key ring.

"Just putting away some stuff. Let's go into the dining room."

"What's wrong with your face?"

He looked in the hall mirror. "What?"

"There's something different about your face. Your eyes are bulging out. Your nose seems larger." Joycelyn took Renato's head in her arms and frowned as she looked at him.

Renato pulled his head free and shook it as he moved closer to the mirror. "You're dreaming. There's nothing wrong." He moved his hands along his skin like he was getting ready for a shave.

"I think I know your face by now."

He continued his inspection. "Yeah, maybe, but I've known it longer." Renato shook his head and walked into the dining room. "Come on in here and let me get you some wine."

The two made up, got caught up, and sat at the dining room table to a meal Renato had prepared.

"When did you start eating your steak rare?" She leaned forward with her fork to turn the cut bloody red side of the meat towards her. "Is that even cooked on the inside?"

"I don't know, today I guess. Tastes better. More wine?"

"You get rid of the mask?"

Renato's stomach tightened. "I put the damn thing in storage." He raised his right hand. "I promise you'll never see it again." He searched her face for a favorable response.

Joycelyn stared at him long and hard, seemingly probing for an answer. "OK." She smiled.

Like a load had been taken off his shoulders, Renato took a shallow breath and smiled. "It's been too long. Let's hit the sack."

After their energies were spent and muscles slackened, Joycelyn rolled on her side. "Where did you come up with all these new tricks? Have you been experimenting with someone else?"

Renato's head pounded as he panted, lying on his back. "What do you mean?"

"Weren't you a bit like a wild beast? You should have seen your face when you, well, you know. I know it's been a few weeks, but really. I would swear you were someone else."

"I didn't realize. Got caught up in the moment." He continued to pant. Images of the mask swirled through his consciousness.

"It was a bit savage. I'm not complaining. Just be careful when you give me those little love bites. I think you drew blood on my neck."

Rrrriiiinnnngggg.

Renato picked up the telephone.

"Renato, I've learned a great deal about the mask. You got some time to discuss this now?"

Diego's call surprised him, but he really didn't have any reason not to talk to him at the moment. "Thanks Diego, go ahead. I'll put you on speaker phone." Renato pushed a button, leaned back to listen...and appreciate the mask and the macuahuitl on his wall.

"Renato, the mask was fashioned to represent a specific individual of mixed Tlaxcaltec and Spanish blood. I learned the mask you have is related to a son, one of several children, a Tlaxcaltec woman bore one of the Spanish soldiers."

"Yes, that wasn't particularly unusual. The conquistadores often took native women as they pleased."

"One of the children was unusual. Cruel to animals as he grew up. About the time he was a young man, the family moved into a Zacatecos village where a number of unmarried women died under unusual circumstances. They were all hacked to death and parts of their bodies were missing."

"Really? A serial killer in the 16th Century?"

Diego challenged. "Why would you think crime has just been invented?"

"Well, you're right."

"Anyway, the villagers eventually figured out this young man was guilty and executed him immediately."

"Sounds like he deserved it."

"He did, but remember this was the time of the Spanish Inquisition. Methods of killing the guilty individuals were quite barbaric."

Renato remembered reading about the methods of torture employed by civilized Spain. And the explicit drawings he found on the Internet.

"Renato, this young man was hacked to death, his head placed on a pike, and the body burned."

"About par for the course in those times."

"Before the young man was executed, he told his victims' fathers and mothers he raped their daughters. He told them he eviscerated their hearts while they were still alive—then ate them. A priest wrote to the Inquisition he told the families their daughters deserved to die. Women were the source of original sin and they all needed to be punished. If that were not enough, he cursed the village and their descendants and vowed to come back and demonize their survivors."

Renato's stomach tightened. "Wow, a bit excessive."

"Well, apparently the villagers thought so too. So before they hacked him to

Horror

death, they cut out his heart, his tongue, broke his teeth, and scalped him alive. And of course they cursed him, his family, and any descendants of the family."

Renato swallowed hard and held his breath. Exhaling, he sputtered, "I thought scalping was only in the American West?"

"Not when the Mexican indigenous tribes wanted to use the scalp to create a mask."

Renato sat up straight and looked at the mask on his wall, eyes widening. "You mean…."

"Wait, it gets worse. The Zacatecos villagers forced the man's Tlaxcaltec family to fashion a mask out of an unburned section of zompantle wood used in the fire. And yes, they used the hair. The young men of his family were forced to wear the mask in a pageant. The object was to warn young women about the dangers of associating with the Spanish. They would threaten the young women with a macuahuitl. By the end of the play, the villagers would ridicule the Tlaxcaltec family member wearing the mask."

Renato sat in total silence. Bass drumbeats pounded in his ears. Sweat soaked his brow, torso and shirt. His body started to tremble and shake.

"You still there?"

"I suppose they hacked him to death with a macuahuitl." His neck hurt. He rolled his shoulders forward and gritted his teeth. *Mouth dry–like it's been used as a dustbin.* His body flushed with warmth starting at his feet and rising up his torso.

"Naturally. The macuahuitl was their weapon of choice. The villagers held theater for many years until the young Tlaxcaltec re-enactors began to meet mysterious endings. Many committed suicide, some went mad, and others disappeared. Some escaped to join the Oñate expedition in New Mexico. Of course, the Zacatecos people all disappeared as a distinct tribe."

Again, Renato was speechless. His eyes were swelling. *They feel like they're going to pop out of my head.* Bright flashes of light exploded in his brain. As he looked at the mask and the macuahuitl, he realized his vision was altered. The top of his view was normal but about one-third the way down the vertical picture in his brain, the view blurred. Like cheese melting in the hot sun. The entire image in his head abruptly swirled right ninety degrees. It extended across a third of his horizontal plane. The photo in his brain then dropped directly down to the bottom of the picture. Like Salvador Dali's painting with melting watches drooping from boxes, trees, and figures. Renato could not grasp which way was up or which way was down. He had no sense of balance and grasped the edge of the desk. His whole body quivered. His chest heaved in great spasms.

"Renato, you understand you now have this exact same mask? You might also be a descendent of the same Spanish conquistador who fathered that killer. You need to get rid of that mask!"

Renato's stomach wrenched. He clenched his jaw and fought back the tightness in his chest and throat—and the overwhelming nausea and taste of bile. He forced open his teeth and started panting with shallow gasps of warm air.

Renato sensed the metallic taste of blood. He smiled as his nostrils flared, and he took large, deep lungsful of warm air.

The young man turned to face the mirror. He held up the mask in front of his face. He had to lean his head forward to get his face to fit into the hollowed-out back of the mask. He could smell the fresh paint. The mask still had the odor of the flames from when they put the mask into the fire to burn off the rough edges. The young man shook his head, then his entire body, as he molded his face to the inside of the hollowed-out back of the mask. The wood was still too rough–it rubbed his skin. *Why do they make me wear this?* As he became more comfortable with the mask, the black hair hanging over his scalp tickled the back of his neck. He adjusted the mask. *Now I can see through the slits.* His body tensed. His breath ceased. He realized his skin was now tingling. He sensed a tickling sensation from the back of his neck down into his bare chest and back up into his face. He looked directly ahead and realized he could see himself in a very clear mirror unlike any they had in the village. Then he saw them. *The eyes...the eyes...the eyes....*

The young man ripped the mask from his face and stared at the mirror. His skin hurt and his eyes felt like they would pop from his head. He put the mask back on and repeated this same process a half dozen times. Each time more frantic. Each time the smell of paint and the fire increased. The young man's throat tightened with each repetition until he let the mask dangle in his left hand. He was transfixed by the image in the mirror.

"Honey, you home?"

The young man heard a woman make some noises in the distance and walk towards him. Her feet made a strange sharp sound on the floor.

"Honey, you in here?"

He watched her enter the room.

"Aaaaaahhhhhhhhhhh!" she screamed and collapsed.

The young man observed himself in the mirror. *The eyes...the eyes...the eyes.* He tried to turn away, but his muscles wouldn't obey. His head spun back to stare at...*the eyes.* The center of the eyes had the color of a bird's egg. The very center

Horror

was dark black. He felt a surge of strength and pleasure– just like when…. The whites were dirty and looked older than his age. *The eyes.* They bulged noticeably from his face. Large black lashes ringed his lids. The eyes were wide open and dominated the face. *The eyes…the eyes…the eyes.*

He saw his face in the mirror.

He saw the mask dangling from his left hand.

Again, he saw his face.

Again, he saw the mask in his left hand.

The mask was his face.

His blood surged. As he took in a deep breath, heat rose into to his cheeks.

He put the mask back on the peg on the wall.

The young man stared in the mirror at the image of the mask that was now his face.

The young man turned towards the wall where he hung the mask.

He took down the macuahuitl from its mounting.

He walked towards the woman.

All these women deserve to be punished.

El asesino swung the macuahuitl through the air. It swooshed with the same "shlock" sound made when a guillotine falls.

The young man smiled and raised the macuahuitl over his head….

The End

Jim Tritten is an award-winning author who resides in a small New Mexico village with his Danish artist/author wife and five cats. He has published four books and hundreds of chapters, articles, and reports. Jim was a frequent speaker at many conferences and has seen his work translated into Russian, French, Spanish, and Portuguese.

Redemption Dog
HMC

Humphrey breathed in the smell of mud mixed with dog faeces and cringed. 'Lovely.' His dog, Albert, stood from his defecating crouch and scratched at the grass and dirt, looking quite pleased with himself. 'I've got no dog bags.' Humphrey searched through his fanny pack. He scoured the park for a *doggy poop bag zone*. When he made his way there, he swiped at the half-torn, plastic bag. 'Last one, as well,' he huffed. 'Good one, Albert. Why can't you shit at home?'

A lady throwing a ball with her Border Collie had been watching him. The Collie barked at the speeding ball and returned it to his master, as quickly as if it were a live grenade in need of another throw. Humphrey felt a twinge of guilt about the poo, and hurried away with Albert in tow.

'Fancy that,' he said to his dog as they wandered home. 'Me feeling bad about being an irresponsible dog owner. I tell you something, Albert. Before you were around, I did a hell of a lot worse things than leave dog shit in a park.' Albert lifted his head and looked at Humphrey, as if in disbelief. If he'd had eyebrows, he'd have surely raised them. 'You don't believe me?' Humphrey wiped his nose with his sleeve. 'Well, there are things out there not worth taking risks for, Albert. Some things happen that'll mess a man up. Change him for life. Make a man piss himself in his sleep enough times, and he'll change for the better. You bloody best believe it.'

Humphrey made his way to his flat on Wattle Street. He unlocked the door to the smell of ashtrays and old Chinese take-away. Albert made his way in, lapped up some water, turned three times, and made himself comfortable on a pair of old pants.

Humphrey sat on his couch, turned on his television to the honourable Judge Judy, and lit a Peter Jackson Blue. He sat puffing away on his cigarette, but as

Horror

much as he would've liked to zone out, his mind kept wandering back – as it always did – to a dark place.

'Ma,' she said, as if she were right in front of him now. 'Ma.' The baby's fingers spread like a fan and reached for Humphrey. Her little bow lips curled into a smile. She giggled.

'I'm not your ma, wee one. Your ma is dead.' Humphrey had said that to her, as he sat on the floor playing and keeping her company. He remembered it because it had more meaning now. He'd told a toddler her ma was dead, and that was good, because it was going to make Humphrey a very rich man – Humphrey and his friends. She didn't understand what he was saying, anyway.

'No, no.' She shook her head, her little curls bouncing around her face. 'Ma!'

'Stop playing with her!' Bill Watson shouted from the kitchen. 'Don't get attached to the little turd. All right?' Bill slammed down a bag full of groceries. He had the look of a drug-addict. With his big mouth and googly eyes he could've walked right off the set of *The Muppet Show*. A cigarette hung out the side of his mouth. He rustled around his bag for instant coffee, and then moved to boil the kettle.

'He's right, Humphrey. Move away from her.' Myers nodded from his permanent spot on the couch. In contrast to Bill, his wide arse filled up the recliner. 'You'll only make it harder, buddy,' he said. He chugged on a beer.

'Being drunk on the job makes it harder, too, Myers.' Humphrey turned away. It was harder, though. It was somehow so much harder than usual, and Humphrey couldn't understand why. 'I'm just playing with her. She's the littlest we've ever taken.'

Myers leaned forward on the couch. It squeaked under his weight. He turned the football down on the television, just as the kettle made itself known with the type of white noise that'd put a baby to sleep. 'She's worth more than every kid we've skyjacked put together,' said Myers, pointing at the baby with the mouth of his beer. 'Daddy will pay a fortune for this one.' He chuckled.

'Exactly,' said Bill from the kitchen, shouting over the noise of the kettle. 'Plus with wifey dead, this monkey's all he has left. Well, 'til we came along. A man wit nofing will give you everyfing, ay!' Bill's cockney accent showed up when he got overexcited.

Humphrey pulled a face at the baby and she smiled. The smell of coffee wafted into the living room as Bill poured the steaming water into his mug. He then made his way over to the dining table which squeezed four around it on a good day. It was covered with printed-out maps, a new phone, and several other bits and pieces that were none of Humphrey's business. He was the scout – the potential finder. This one was his pick, and Bill was right, she was the perfect score. What daddy wouldn't pay a king's ransom for this one? They could be done in less than 24 hours.

'Leave her.' Bill persisted.

'I'm just making sure she's happy!' Humphrey turned and threw a teddy at Bill. It flew past his head and hit the wall behind him. 'She's too young to identify us in a line-up, so shut the hell up and leave us alone.'

'You soft prick.' Bill shook his head.

'It's all right, angel.' Humphrey stroked her little hand. It was so soft. 'You're going to be all right.' Humphrey lifted up a caterpillar toy and made it dance for her. She giggled. 'Ma!'

Humphrey frowned.

Humphrey woke to the baby crying. He threw off his bed covers and went to stand. A great pressure hit his chest. He was thrown back down onto the bed and hands grabbed his throat, strangling him. It was too dark to see, but Humphrey thought of Bill, come to get rid of him and keep Humphrey's part of the kidnap money.

Humphrey struggled and thrashed about as hard as he could. He punched the air but couldn't connect. Tears came to his eyes. He grabbed at his throat. It was on fire! The scrawny bastard was strong. *Get off me*! He shrieked in his head. Humphrey thought he'd die. This was it. The baby cried louder.

The hands released.

Humphrey gasped. He held his throat and breathed sweet relief. He jumped over to switch on his lamp and catch Bill standing at the end of his bed, but there was no one there.

The baby stopped crying.

Ma...

A stomach-turning scream came from the next room. This time it was Bill. Humphrey got up. He pulled out his Old Fox hunting knife from the side drawer, ran to the hallway, and flicked the switch. He turned the handle to Bill's room. It was locked. 'Bill! What's going on!' Humphrey shouted. Bills screamed again. It had to be Myers. 'Myers, what are you doing to him!'

Myers showed up next to Humphrey. 'It's not me, Humphs.'

'Then who is it!' Humphrey put his knife in his pocket and thrashed against the door. 'Bill!' The screaming turned to gurgling – like water down a drain. Humphrey imagined Bill being strangled with his Muppet eyes bulging from

Horror

his head.

Myers pushed the door with him. Together they beat their hands and shook the handle to get to Bill. Myers stopped. 'We can't open it.' He was panicking. 'Get a fuckin' hatchet, right?'

'What?' Myers hurried into the living room before Humphrey could tell him to stop and calm down. Humphrey stood at the door, thinking. Bill was quiet. 'Bill?' he said. There was no response. 'You all right, buddy?' Still nothing. Whoever got to him … got to him proper. *What in God's name is happening?*

Humphrey walked into the kitchen. Myers had gone outside and returned with the hatchet. 'We don't need that,' Humphrey said. 'Just get a screwdriver. I'll take the door handle off. I'm not looking forward to finding out what just went on in that room.' Humphrey rubbed his sore neck. It was still burning from his run-in with thin air. Myers stood there, stunned, like a docile kid given too many instructions. 'Pull yourself together, Myers! Put down that bloody thing, and go in and check on the baby. She's upset.'

Myers nodded, but didn't budge. The hatchet in his hand swung in the air nearly hitting him in the face. Myers' eyes grew large. He inhaled sharply.

'What are you doing?' Humphrey frowned.

'I'm not doing it!' The hatchet swung again. This time it turned and landed in Myers' left arm. He screamed louder than the baby, and tried to pull the blade out.

'Leave it in!' Humphrey shouted, hands raised in protest. Blood poured down Myers' arm. Myers didn't listen. He pulled the blade out. Humphrey thought the blood looked a strange colour. More black than red. Myers took the handle with both hands, and thrust it into his chest over and over. 'MYERS!' Humphrey wanted to go to him, but he stood back, and watched as some unseen forced hacked away at his friend. The scream he heard from Bill was much like the one Myers made now. Humphrey grabbed the counter to steady himself. *Stay back*, he told himself.

Myers was on the floor in a pool of blood, hatchet in hand, and chest burst open like a red-bowed, birthday piñata.

Still, the baby cried.

Humphrey swayed. His body prickled with fear and he found it hard to move from the spot. The thing that choked him earlier had likely killed both his friends, and it was coming for him next. He stood with his Old Fox knife in his shaking hand. Sweat dripped from his brow as he made his way through the living room. When he looked at the dead body again, his stomach roiled. He threw his knife across the room. He didn't want a repeat stabbing. His heart thumped as if it had made his way up his throat and now sat in his ears.

Humphrey went to pacify the baby. He switched on her light. She was standing in the porta-cot Humphrey had bought at a garage sale four weeks prior. She reached out her hands to Humphrey. Her eyes were like stars in the blackest night – sparkling with both terror and relief at the sight of him.

'It's okay, little one.' Humphrey said. Her face was wet from crying, and as Humphrey picked her up, she snuggled into his chest. He shook. 'I'm more frightened than you, but let's not focus on that, shall we?'

Humphrey turned. A dark, swaying figure stood in the doorway. The baby smiled.

Humphrey froze. The dark thing wavered on the threshold – a hole in the space before him.

'Ma!' The baby reached out to the thing, and giggled.

Humphrey's heart skipped a beat and he'd surely go into cardiac arrest. 'Ma?' he said. 'You're her mother,' Humphrey whispered at the thing. It said nothing, did nothing, just stood and wavered like a wacky, waving inflatable man – the kind they put out the front of car yards.

Come on in, folks!

Humphrey waited for it to enter, but it stayed put, blocking his way out.

'I'm sorry,' Humphrey stammered. 'I'm so sorry for what we've done.' He coughed. He thought he'd vomit, and he swallowed back the lump in his throat. 'I'll fix it,' he said.

I'll fix it. I'll fix it. I'll fix it.

The thing hissed and came into the room. Humphrey's skin crawled as it came towards them. His initial reaction was to cover the baby's head and to protect it. The dark thing slithered up the wall and over Humphrey's head. The baby reached her arms up and laughed again. Humphrey closed his eyes and held his breath. He waited for death – deserved it … welcomed it. Humphrey was a waste of space. He'd known it all his life.

There was a scream from the ceiling.

Humphrey jumped. Then there was silence.

'Ba,' said the baby. 'Bab, bab, ba!'

Humphrey exhaled. He looked up. The thing was gone. He looked down at the girl in his arms. 'I'll fix it,' he said. She snuggled into him again.

'I fixed it, Albert.' Humphrey shifted in his chair as Judge Judy made yet another plaintiff feel worthless and unintelligent. 'Three years for attempted kidnap.' Albert was only pretending to listen. He was trying to sleep. Humphrey sniffed. 'I deserved worse. Took little Bridget to the police station myself that night. She was returned to her daddy. It was suspicious, you know, Albert. Of course it was. Two men taking their own lives like that – one with a machete

Horror

from his own cupboard, and one with a hatchet from the yard. But Myers and Bill had a pretty messed-up track record, and dealing was one of them. Soon as they think you're a druggie, anything goes, you know? My lucky arse, hey? Three years. Three years, a shit-load of therapy, and a dog. A dog recommended by my shrink lady to keep me company when I'm lonely.' Humphrey snuffed out his cigarette. Albert sneezed. 'That's you, Albert. I'll tell you what – being worried about a shit in a park – that's the life for me.'

The End

I'm **Hayley**. I live on the Goldy (Australia), teach awesomely funny high school kids, have two hilarious (and mental) toddlers, am engaged to a motorbike-loving Viking, and sometimes I write. I write for no other reason but to express myself. And if you're here reading my writing, that's my very cool bonus.

I blog about asylum seekers, gay rights, tattooed professionals, robot dancing, baby poo, and so on … you know, the juicy stuff. I'm sometimes serious, but mostly not. I write poems, short stories, and novels (three to date) which has surpassed any goal I ever had. Go team. Aaaaaaand that's about it. No need to waffle, unless it's Belgian. Or Chinese.

PEACE

HMC

Visit Hayley at www.hmcwriter.com

Quietly, Ross

Kerry E.B. Black

It waited in Ross's closet, as it did most nights, hidden from the light, its steely nails scratching even during the brightest of days. At night, the door made a slow, high-pitched screech and it scuffled out, red eyes glowing. Moonlight glinted off of the strong, sharp teeth. Its snake-like tail whispered behind its plump, gray body.

Ross huddled under the covers, praying for protection. His brow gleamed with sweat in the golden half-light of the smiley face night light. His hands ached from clutching the covers to his chin. He dared not cry out. It would know he was awake if he screamed.

Ross held his breath. It came closer, its pin sharp claws catching on the bedding as it climbed. He ducked under the covers, a cocoon of sanctuary. He felt the thing's weight pressing on his chest as it scurried toward his face. He hunched his shoulders and drew up his knees, hoping his smallness might escape notice.

He heard sniffling sounds, felt the thing digging at his covers. He quaked and tightened his grip on the rough cotton blankets. He held the blanket taut, his only defense against the invader his parents refused to believe existed. Ringing deafened his right ear. His ear always rang when the thing drew close. It squeaked. Ross pressed his trembling lips together to keep from answering in kind.

The pressure changed on the bed and a thump announced that it was on the ground, scampering among his playthings, hiding in baskets, chewing beloved books. Ross released a breath he hadn't known he'd held. He shook with terror.

Why won't mom and dad believe me? I'm so scared.

He whimpered and waited for morning to brighten his room and chase the rodent back to the closet where it nested in the back wall.

Horror

When the alarm sounded, Ross sighed. He nestled into the comforts of his bed. With daybreak, he could sleep without fear of the rat.

"Time to get up! Get dressed."

"Please, I'm so tired." Terrifying evenings exacted a toll. He felt queasy, unsteady.

"Up," said his father, annoyance reverberating through his deep voice.

Ross groaned. When he reached for his clothes, he stumbled. Dizziness overtook him, and he careened like a drunken pirate into the edge of his desk. "Argh!"

"Come on, chum, suck it up. We have to get you to Uncle Tim's. We're going to be late for work if we don't go soon."

Ross whimpered but got ready, nursing the growing bump on the back of his head.

Uncle Tim moved using a wheelchair. He watched Ross during workdays when school was out. He had wild hair, wise eyes, and a smile reluctant to intrude on Ross's pervasive melancholy.

"Hey, Ross Sauce," Uncle Tim greeted.

Ross fist bumped, then retired to a customary corner of a dark, stained couch to read the latest "American Heroes" comic. The tiny black letters swam before his eyes, and Ross fell asleep.

"Wake up, Ross." Uncle Tim shook his shoulders, fingers digging with insistence.

Ross propped himself up. His comic slipped to the shag carpet. Ross rubbed the sleep sand from his eyes with trembling hands. His temples pounded, his heart raced, and it hurt to move his eyes. The air cooled the sweat that dripped from his hairline.

Uncle Tim leaned as far from his chair as he could without falling. He stared with red-rimmed eyes at his nephew. "Dude, what the hell was that? You scared the – are you okay now?"

Ross licked his cracked lips. "I'm okay. What happened?"

Uncle Tim relaxed, but his gaze never left his nephew's face. "Beats me, but that was some trip, kid." He reached into the pocket of his black leather vest for a pack of cigarettes. Uncle Tim's hands shook as he took a drag, exhaling smoke like a dragon. He tipped his head to the right, scrutinizing the boy. He blinked, rapid repetitions like gunfire, then asked, "You want to talk about it?"

Ross cleared his throat. He refused to burden his uncle. "No. I just want a drink."

"Bet you do," Uncle Tim muttered and nodded. He tousled Ross's hair. Cigarette smoke snaked around the two.

"You know the soda's in the fridge."

That evening, Ross delayed the inevitable by dragging out evening rituals. Teeth shone from the ministrations of paste and floss. Shower, comb hair, lay out clothes for the morning showed him a responsible man of ten, even if it was only an illusion.

"What on earth are you doing now, son?" asked his mother.

"Just tidying up my room."

"It is bed time now. Get to sleep."

He bit his lip, trembling. His heart raced faster as his mind searched for an escape. He ran his hand across his smooth chin.

I need a distraction. What will work on Mom?

"Mom, do you think a girl will ever like me?"

She sat on his bed, a mother behind beautiful, brown eyes. "Of course, honey. Why would you worry about such things?"

He shrugged his shoulders, fighting an urge to close heavy eyes. If he gave in, she would leave. He did not want to be left.

She put a hand beneath his chin and looked into his eyes.

"You are so handsome, with your father's strong jawline and your grandmother's dark hair." She studied his face, concern playing with the crow's feet at the corners of her eyes. "You haven't been sleeping again, have you?"

He was too tired to deny the truth.

"Please tell me what is bothering you."

A shiver ripped up his spine like an electrical impulse. He stole a glance at the closet, then begged his mother, "Not in here. Can we talk in the other room, please?"

Her mouth pinched in, as though blocking words. She traced a hand along the side of his face, and nodded. "Just for a couple of minutes though."

He bolted from the room, closing his door behind them.

"I told you, there's a rat in the closet in that room," he whispered as they hurried to the sofa.

She embraced him. "Honey, I love you so much, and I know that you are scared, but please listen to reason. There is no rat. I had an exterminator inspect the entire house. There are no rodents at all. Not even a mouse or hamster."

He shrugged out of her hug. "He must've missed it, Mom. The thing comes out every night. It climbs on my bed and sits on my chest. It is huge and disgusting."

She looked ceiling-ward, as though patience might fall like manna from the heights. "Ross, Honey, I don't know what to tell you."

"Maybe it hid in the wall?"

Her lips pressed into a thin line, and swollen eyelids veiled concerned eyes.

Horror

She took a steadying breath before continuing in a level voice. "I had them check the walls, love. No rat."

Mom would not help. His neck and shoulders stiffened, and his ears rang. "I'm not making this up."

"You've always been imaginative, my love. You probably dreamed it." She hugged him. "Now please get some sleep."

He lowered his chin and closed his eyes to think. He willed an emerging headache away.

I need a plan.

He nodded off on the couch beside his mother.

"Go to sleep. You are so tired that you're falling asleep here."

"Hey, that's a great idea! Can I sleep here tonight? Please mom?"

Her breath huffed in a frustrated sigh. "Fine, just for the love of all, go to sleep."

"Can you get my pillows for me, please?"

"Seriously?"

"Never mind. Just stay here while I get them."

He retrieved his blanket and pillow.

She tucked him in with a kiss on the forehead and smiled. "I've not done that in a long time." She pushed his hair back from his cheek. "Don't forget to say your prayers, darling."

He nodded, though he'd not prayed since the rat started haunting his dreams a couple of weeks earlier.

Ross knew his parents disliked night-time disturbances. He followed rules, comfortable with their structure. If he did something wrong, acted out, he punished himself with guilt and confessed for relief. Breaking this rule drained him, but terror gripped him, and he did not know what else to do.

Lack of sleep hurt his eyes and made them look puffy. His appetite disappeared and so did his waist. His clothes hung on him like hand-me-downs. His dark hair defied efforts of control, springing skyward like an indomitable spirit.

He rubbed his chin, a calming technique from his early childhood. He steeled himself before turning the handle to his parents' room.

He whispered, "Mom, mom, please wake up. I am so scared and don't know what to do."

She stirred.

"Please, Mom, I need you."

"Ross," her voice sounded rough, as though dredged from a gravel pit. "This needs to stop."

Desperation inspired his words. He quaked with reaction, sick to his stomach, exhausted but terrified to sleep. "I know. I do." He fought tears that collected in a lump high in his throat. The pressure in his head pushed at his eyes from their sockets.

She sat up with a grunt. She swung her feet from the covers to waiting slippers and grabbed a soft pink robe draped across her slipper chair. She cast an envious glance at his sleeping father, then grabbed her son's hand and pulled him from the bedroom.

In the living room, she yawned. "What is it now, son?"

"The rat," he hissed. "It came into the hallway."

Her eyes narrowed. "Where is it now?"

"I don't know. I heard it scuffling along, so I ran."

She looked around at the glare of every lamp in the room. She turned one off, then another.

"What are you doing?" His voice pitched high in hysteria.

"You can't sleep with all of these lights on, and we both need sleep."

"Please, Mom, leave them on."

She stopped, hand outstretched toward a desk lamp. "Why?"

"It doesn't like the light, I think."

Her arm dropped with a *smack* to her side. She shook her head, and frowned. "Fine. One light on, but you have to go to sleep."

He nodded, staring down the hallway led to his room. His voice sounded small when he said, "Mom, why won't it leave me alone?"

She sat beside him and looked down the hall as well. Worry trumped tired, he guessed. He put his arm around her shoulders and inhaled the homey scent of furniture polish and face soap. She hummed a tune from cradle days when sleep brought dreams of adventures. Her warmth and nearness comforted him, and he slept at last.

The morning brought the usual rush for readiness. Hurried breakfast, hasty preparations, and then he dashed to catch the school bus. As he ran out the door, he overheard his father say, "You need to stop babying him. No more sleeping on the couch. Got it?"

On the school bus, he rested his head against the cool, smudged glass for the trip and thought. His headache felt better since he managed to sleep.

School bored him, but he earned good grades. He'd become quiet and reserved

Horror

since the rat began its night time visits. He drifted to sleep, head pillowed on hands, at his desk at times. At recess, Tammy Hanson and the Pepper twins ran screaming from a corner of the fenced exercise yard. A group of boys investigated the area. Ross tagged along. "Ewww, what is that thing?" Bob O'Malley asked.

Jake Simsick grabbed a stick and poked at the brown fur. Ross edged closer, peering between the boys' shoulders. The animal wiggled independent of the prodding. "Uughh!" Jake dropped the stick and backed away. Ross retrieved the wood and touched it to the rodent, turning it onto its feet.

"It is a rat," he exclaimed. The boys moved closer, following his lead. The thing squeaked. Ross' shoulders twitched and his stomach knotted. With a quick thrust, he speared it. The animal squeaked again and slowly turned beady dark eyes. Ross felt ill. He raised the stick again and smacked the rat on its shoulder, its stomach, and its rump. He continued, tears streaming down his face.

The boys around him muttered, but Ross remained in his own world. Only the rat mattered. His ears rang. He sneered, smashing it with his stick until a teacher pulled him away.

She took the stick and threw it over the fence. Kneeling before him, she smoothed Ross' hair and wiped his tears. "Are you okay, Ross?" Her voice sounded as though it traveled through a heavy, spring fog. "Come on, let's get you to the nurse."

He lay on a cot with a thermometer under his tongue, wrapped in a scratchy olive-green blanket. The teacher and nurse conferred behind a screen. Their words sounded like bees buzzing. He closed his eyes. The ringing in his ears brought the headache back. His neck and shoulders stiffened and cramped. *How many times did I hit that thing?*

The nurse removed the thermometer and checked the reading. "That looks normal." Ross knew his temperature was the only thing the nurse found "normal" about Ross. He closed his eyes and slept until his mother collected him.

He came home from school and bounced his backpack onto his bed. He froze when he noticed the open closet door.

"Mom!" he yelled, backing out.

He startled when she touched his shoulders. "Who's been in my room?"

"Me. Come see."

He remained in the hall until she grabbed his hand and pulled him along.

"I sorted out your toys and clothes. It is all much more organized. But best of all, I've re-paneled everything with cedar board. No rat holes. No rats." She straightened a shirt, the hangars tinking like wind chimes. Her satisfied look froze when she saw his face. "Honey, are you alright?"

Why can't she see it?

The rat hunched on a shelf just behind his mother's head, between a box labeled "puzzles" in his mother's handwriting and his junior chemistry kit. It stretched its mouth open, revealing startling, sharp white teeth. Its red eyes glowed, pupil-less, like Hell's embers.

"Mom, turn around."

She looked over her shoulder at her handiwork. "What? What is wrong?"

"There, on the shelf at eye-level, do you see anything – weird?"

He gleaned from her blank expression she saw nothing but a well-organized space.

Am I crazy?

He felt faint. "Mom, I think I need help!" He turned and ran to the bathroom and vomited.

He overheard his mother talking, voice a high-pitched whisper, into her cellular telephone. "Tim, I'm just so worried about him. Oh, would you please? I think that would help. Thank you! You are the best big brother!" She paced with irregular strides, her limp evident in agitation. "We can try. Why don't you come for dinner? Great! I will see you at 6, okay? Thanks again! I love you!"

She slumped into a kitchen chair.

"Mom?"

She jumped. "Ross, I didn't know you were there." She hesitated before asking, "How are you feeling?"

"Fine. Is Uncle Tim coming to dinner?"

She nodded.

"Good."

Ross suspected it was time he confided in Uncle Tim.

He completed his math homework, then helped with dinner preparations. He chopped onions, wiping tears from his eyes.

"Run the onion under the water. That will take away some of the oils that make you tear up."

He did. Mom sliced mushrooms and dropped them in a red-wine sauce. The kitchen filled with good smells. Popovers baked. Meat broiled. Ross's stomach rumbled, anticipating the meal.

"Set the table, love. Use the good plates."

Horror

"Okay, Mom."

He placed the china, the silver clanked atop the linen napkins. He lit the white candle centerpiece and washed up for the meal. When he took his place, Uncle Tim sat opposite him. They enjoyed the meal, and then Ross helped his mom tidy up after.

"Why don't you chat with Uncle Tim?" she suggested. "Show him your room."

Ross shifted his weight from leg to leg and reached for his chin. "Okay," he said.

Uncle Tim wheeled into Ross's room. He looked around. "Mighty neat for a boy's room," he said. He perused the titles on the bookshelf. He had given Ross many of them as presents.

Ross perched on his bed like a gargoyle, silent, stiff and alert.

"So, what's going on, Ross Sauce? Your Mom's worried about you."

Ross barely lifted his shoulder in response.

Uncle Tim wheeled closer to the bed, orienting his chair toward the window and the closet like his nephew. "Dude, I can't help if you don't tell me what's going on."

Ross glanced at his uncle, then resumed his contemplation.

"Okay, your Mom said there's something bothering you in the closet. Show me."

Ross moved, arms tight to his body, head low, his eyes never leaving the corner of the room with its brown wood door and antique knob. Uncle Tim's chair whistled as he made his way there. He turned the handle and threw open the door with a thump against the wall.

Inside, well-organized objects and tidy clothes hung in the cedar-lined space. Ross backed behind his Uncle's chair and pointed over his shoulder with a shaking index finger. He whispered, "Do you see it? There, on the middle shelf?"

Uncle Tim shivered. "What is it, Ross?"

He drew closer to his uncle, finding comfort in the warmth emanating from his shoulder. He whispered, afraid to draw the thing's attention. "A rat. It is right there." The rat opened its blood-red mouth and showed sharp teeth.

Uncle Tim pulled Ross to his side. Ross dragged his feet. He wanted to be brave for his uncle, but his insides quaked. He felt the urge to pee.

"Ross, whatever it is, you have to face it, man, no matter how hard."

Tears raced down his face, and a solid ball formed high in his throat. The shaking grew to convulsions. Uncle Tim pulled the boy onto his lap, holding him close. Ross continued to stare, barely blinking, into the shadowy alcove.

"What the hell is it? Tell me, Ross. What is the rat?"

Ross looked his Uncle in the eye, his voice a skeletal whisper. The rat screamed, trying to prevent the words. Once the emotional flood-gates opened, they rushed with snot and tears, dripping feelings of guilt and disgust.

"He touches me. He said I could never tell, that he'd hear me. He pushes me into the closet. He said no one would believe me…"

Uncle Tim held his nephew, stiffening with each disclosure. His stony face revealed nothing, but his eyes raged. When Ross finished, Uncle Tim said, "Listen to me. I knew a rat like that. He did bad things to me in my closet, too."

Ross' eyes widened. He licked his lips, feeling parched. He whispered, "Who was it? Who was the rat, Uncle Tim?"

Uncle Tim blinked back tears. "Your grandfather."

Ross gasped. Chills prickled his arms, and he felt sick.

Uncle Tim nodded. "In life, sometimes bad things happen, and sometimes monsters do more than live in your closet." He kissed the top of Ross' head. "The damned rat is dead. It died of old age. It can't hurt anyone now. It can't hurt you anymore."

The rat blurred as Ross' tears poured unchecked over his chin and dripped to his t-shirt. When he finished, exhausted, trembling, nauseated, the rat vanished for good.

The End

Kerry E.B. Black lives along the Allegheny River in Pennsylvania where fog snakes thick tendrils through fancies. Possessed of an active imagination, Kerry finds inspiration everywhere. However, she's most inspired by the diversity of nature, the wistfulness of dreams, and the energy of her large, vibrant family.

Please follow Kerry on Twitter @BlackKerryblick and

www.facebook.com/authorKerryE.B.Black

All He Loved

Kelly Haas Shackelford

Henry Walker turned his face to the wind. The summer storm lashed at his freshly shaved skin. Tears burnt his eyes, but not from the salt water of the roaring ocean tumbling around him. Those tears welled up watching the familiar wisp of smoke rising from the black depths. He lifted his heavy legs up and pushed deeper into the frothing waves. His burden laden with grief, he screamed. As was his deal with the demon, he was now her killer.

Twenty years ago, when their boat capsized, the water demon had saved his family's life. His wife, pregnant with their only child, had been knocked out. Struggling for hours to keep them both afloat, Henry's arms gave way and they began to sink. The black demon rushed up from her pit and gave him a choice: she would save their lives, but in twenty years, Henry would become her slave. He would have to claim twelve souls for her. In despair, Henry accepted the deal with one condition: that the haggard demon could not harm all he loved.

Through countless nights, Henry wondered who his twelve tokens of damnation would be. Would it be a mother playing with her child, or would it be the child? Someone's wife? Someone's son?

Tormenting his soul, guilt consumed him. Determined to make his second chance count, he became a pillar of society. Driving contrition sustained him in his quest to save as many souls as he could before the coin flipped.

"I'm ready," Henry said, water pounding his chest. Ignoring the warning cries of a stranger on the beach, Henry pushed on into the fury of the ocean. He knew, if he broke the deal, she would claim all he loved, and that was a price too high for him to pay.

Dancing around him amid the now torrential rain, the demon ran her long, twisted fingers through her new plaything's drenched brown hair. Her black skin shimmered from the hundreds of worms latched onto her. Their fat bodies moved in a morbid symphony. Opening her mouth, her forked tongue slithered out, touching Henry's cheek.

Revulsion choked Henry. His brilliant blue eyes dimmed, knowing he was hers to do with as she pleased: to drown, to torture, or to leave alone to wallow in his own self-pity.

"Henry, I claim your soul until you have delivered twelve to me." She hissed in his ear. "You get to decide on eleven souls. I give you the description of what flesh I am hungry for. You deliver my meal. However, the twelfth soul is completely mine to choose."

"I will pick all twelve," Henry shouted.

"Meat doesn't make the rules." She spat at him. "Try my patience further wormling, and I will slaughter all you love."

Drooping, Henry's shoulder's dipped beneath the waves as the salty water filled his mouth, filling his lungs in bitter defeat.

Two years later, Henry drowned his first soul. After the demon had whispered the sex and age of the soul, sorrow filled Henry. Still, he had to claim her meal, or she would claim all he loved. His wife and his daughter could not pay for his deal.

It was the first storm of the season, and the demon was hungry. Waiting for the prey to wade out, Henry hid beneath the waves.

The heavy-set man ignored his wife's pleas to return to shore. It would be hours before the hurricane hit. Laughing at her, he plodded further out, wanting to feel the power of the wind whip against his face before heading back to the safety of his home.

Upon seeing the man, anger urged Henry to snatch him and take him underneath the waves to the demon as he recalled the man's trial. Thanks to an expensive legal team, the man had gotten off, while six kids were forced to piece back their childhood.

Losing that trial and having to tell those six victims he was sorry had been a bitter point in Henry's otherwise stellar career as a district attorney.

Snaking his long fingers around the man's thick calf, Henry jerked. Fighting the water rushing into his lungs, the man panicked, opening his mouth. Fear filled every cell in him. His lungs burnt for oxygen as the water stole his soul. His shouts were drowned out and his lungs were crushed. Condemned and consumed by a jury of one.

Horror

Trembling, Henry threw the dead man at the demon's open mouth. Her pointed teeth sunk into the meat as Henry swam away. Tears of disgust flowed down his face, choking him as he wondered who the bigger monster was: the molester or himself?

Henry stopped weeping after his fifth drowning. There were no tears left. A coldness blackened his heart. Numb to the world, Henry haunted the bottom of the ocean. Just like the demon, as her slave, he was unable to leave the water. Months, years, would roll by before she would call, while he hid at the bottom, listening to the lullaby of kids playing. He often wondered where his own daughter Mary was, and if she had children of her own now.

He had insisted that his daughter stay away from the ocean, drilling its danger into her. How it could suck a soul under. He often wondered if she disregarded his lessons when he walked into the ocean to never return again.

It was the day of his ninth drowning that he considered killing his own dead soul. Picking up a broken, jagged green shard of glass, he flipped it over and over through his fingers, longing to plunge its salvation deep. But he knew to take the coward's way out would mean all he loved would pay.

On that sunny day, laughter filled the beach. Lurking under the waves, Henry people watched until the demon whispered, "Girl, sixteen years old."

"No," he screamed, causing a ripple to form in the calm waters.

"Girl, age sixteen, or all you love, Henry. Your choice. I demand my payment before the sun sets." She laughed and rushed back to her pit.

Watching, waiting all day, Henry knew he would have to take a child or lose all he loved.

Minutes before the sun slid under the horizon and his condemnation sealed, Henry saw her. He tried not to look at the blonde curls that reminded him of his own Mary. He tried not to hear her giggles, but they filled him.

Before he could change his mind, he slid under the peaceful water, waiting for a wave. As the water rushed in, Henry gripped her ankles and pulled her under. He tried to block out the pleadings of her mother for someone to save her daughter as he drug the girl to the demon.

He prayed he'd rot in hell for that act.

Ten years after he had walked into the ocean, Henry owed only one more soul. Since the teenage girl, he had tried to stay away from beaches with kids for fear the demon would make him claim another child.

Dread filled him as he felt her hunger deep in his bones; soon the demon would need to be fed. She circled around him, licking her lips.

"Mary Walker." She whispered in his ear.

"You said you wouldn't take someone I loved," he shouted back.

"No, Henry, you ought to learn to listen better. I said I wouldn't take all you loved."

Fury spewed out of Henry as the sea around him frothed with his anger. The waves turned to battering rams, threatening to destroy anyone in their wake. Henry opened his mouth, screaming. The winds swirled in vicious circles, drawing their energy from his anger.

"Congrats, Henry, you just spawned your first hurricane," she shouted and laughed. Hissing against the storm, her words rocked him.

"Take my soul and leave hers," he begged.

"My dear, dear Henry. I already own your soul," she said and grinned.

"I will not do it."

"I will take all you love, Henry. Your two grandchildren included," she hissed, swimming in circles around him.

Henry wondered how she knew he had grandchildren. He wondered if they were boys or girls, and if Mary had told them about their grandfather. Instinctively he knew Mary would want her babies saved. Burning through him like gut-rot shine, sorrow took hold. He knew what he had to do. He had to save Mary's babies. He had to murder his beloved Mary.

Two days later, he saw her. Gleaming in the sunlight, her golden hair bounced around her tanned face. She looked just like her mother.

Rocking back and forth under the waves, Henry cried in agony. How could he take his own child? Wishing a thousand times over he had died that day instead of making the deal, his body shook, knowing the sins of the father would be paid by the child. History had proven it over and over. Yet, failing to grasp its meaning all those years ago, it's cruel lesson had come to bear on Henry.

Watching his two young granddaughters play in the sand, Henry's heart sunk even further. Mary never left their side until dusk, showering them with attention. The girls' father had arrived and was watching them.

Stepping carefully, Mary waded into the water. It was the first time since her father's death that she had been in the ocean, but she thought it was time to bury her own past and face her fears.

Horror

"Oh, Daddy," she whispered, her legs trembling as she missed her beloved father.

Wrapping his shaking fingers around her leg, Henry tugged, pulling her under. Staring into his face, shock filled her eyes as the salt water burnt them. Screams of torment escaped his lips as she swung her arms at him, fighting for her life.

Recalling how he held her all day when she was born, how he taught her to ride a bicycle, and to throw a punch, despair chocked him. Bitter-sweet memories flooded into him as he hung on to her, for he knew if he let go, the demon would claim her babies

"Henry, give her to me," the demon hissed, licking her lips, eager to consume her prey.

"I'm sorry," Henry cried out to Mary. "Don't let the girls in the ocean, or she will kill them." Releasing Mary, he dove onto the demon, driving her down to the ocean floor. Hidden strength welled up in him, pouring out as he fought hard to save his child's life. Battling to keep the demon pinned, Henry fought through the pain of the acid she was spitting onto him, his flesh boiling off in chucks. Yet, he held on. No amount of pain could tear Henry off her. He knew Hell and feared it no more.

Struggling to catch her breath, Mary surfaced and looked around. Wading out into the waves, her youngest daughter held onto her father's hand. Grinning, she waved at her mother.

Shouting and waving for them to get out of the water, fear filled Mary. Stroke after stroke, she fought through her burning limbs as she headed towards the shore, afraid to look up to see if her child was still there or if she had been taken by the demon.

Daring to look up, her heart froze as a wave hit her daughter, knocking her down. "No," Mary shouted, fighting against the waves harder to get to her child. Hitting the shore, she screamed. Her daughter was not standing there. Frantically, she looked around.

Burying her sister in the sand, her youngest daughter grinned at her. Jumping up, Mary dashed to the girls and fell down. Like a starving dog digging for a bone, she desperately dug the sand out from around her oldest daughter. Upon clearing the small tomb, she snatched the girls up and ran, leaving behind their beach wares. They would never need such items again.

Years later, lurching over Henry's rotting bones, the demon laughs at his trapped soul, forever anchored to the ocean floor. Gliding by him, she taunts

him, waiting on the day when all he loves ventures into the water, and she can claim what is hers.

The End

Kelly Haas Shackeflord has had over 70 pieces published in various venues. By day she is a kitty rescuer and by night she is a Romance Enhancement Specialist. To find out more about kittyhood or her writing, please friend or subscribe to her on Facebook: Kelly Haas Shackelford.

Clandestine

T.D. Harvey

A whispered voice slipped through her shroud of sleep. "I'm not Owen."

Elaine's heart seized. In the darkness of the bedroom she could see a man she thought she knew crouched to meet her, face to eerie, smiling face. She screamed and shot up in bed.

"Lainey, Lainey, it's me," Owen said, laughing and reaching out to her. "It's me. Oh, I'm sorry. It was just a joke."

Elaine's heart restarted itself, pounding in her chest while tears streamed down her ashen face. Her breathing came fast and shallow and sweat broke out across her goose-bumped skin. She looked at her husband of six years, partner of twelve, and fought to restore calm.

"A joke?" Fury overtook all other emotions as her husband tried to placate her whilst laughing at his own trick. "Joke? You bastard!"

"I'm sorry, Lainey," he said in a gentle voice. He stroked her hair and kissed the top of her head. Almost against her will, Elaine's body melted into his.

"Bastard."

"I know."

"You know how much that scares me."

"I know. I'm sorry."

"You know—"

"I do. I'm sorry. It's just…" Owen paused as if trying to find the right words. "It's such a silly fear."

Wrong words.

"Silly? So I'm silly, am I? And that gives you the right to scare the crap out of me?"

"No, baby. No. I just—"

"Wanted to amuse yourself?" She sat up again and pulled away from him.

"You—"

Further recriminations were halted when the bedroom door opened and a small face appeared in the dark. "Mummy, I'm scared. I heard screaming."

Elaine rushed off the bed to her little girl and enveloped her in soft, comforting arms. "It's okay, Little Bug. Mummy had a bad dream, that's all." She glared at Owen.

He joined them on the floor and stroked his daughter's head as he kissed his wife's once more. He whispered another apology into her hair. "I love you, Lainey. I'm so sorry."

Again Elaine melted into his arms, pulling Little Bug—or Lacey, to use her proper name—onto her lap and they stayed there, Elaine singing and Owen rocking the three of them. When the baby began to cry, Elaine took the sleeping Little Bug back to her room whilst Owen checked on their son, Egan.

"He scared me half to death, Bea," Elaine said into the phone as she fed Egan spoons of rusk and milk. In a low voice, head turned from the children, she said, "I woke Little Bug when I screamed. She was so scared."

"I'm okay now, Mummy," Little Bug assured her. The four-year-old had enormous brown eyes encased in long black eyelashes. Her dark brown hair fell in natural ringlets and her skin was soft with a hint of tan. "I'm not scared anymore."

"I know, Little Bug," Elaine answered. Into the phone she said, "I better go. See you later."

Elaine's day consisted of feeding, changing nappies, cleaning, cleaning and more cleaning. She didn't complain, however, because she also got to spend her time with her two beautiful children. In September, Little Bug would be starting school so she didn't want to waste a moment with her smart, funny, gentle and utterly adorable daughter. As for Egan, he was only ten months and she had plenty of time left with him.

"Hello," Owen called from the front door.

"Daddy!" Little Bug flew from her seat at the kitchen table and raced to her father. When she returned, she was riding his shoulders, a huge grin lighting her round face.

"What did you forget?" Elaine raised an eyebrow to her husband who should have been on his morning commute to the office in London.

"Nothing," Owen said with a grin. "Took the day off to spend with my girls and the big man over there." From behind his back he whipped out a large bouquet

of flowers. Lilies, roses and so many other flowers Elaine couldn't name were wrapped in cellophane and purple ribbons.

"Owen—"

"I wanted to, okay? After last night."

Elaine shook her head and smiled at her husband. She kissed him and took the flowers.

The family spent the day at the beach. They played in the water, built sand castles, ate ice-creams and laughed all day. Little Bug and Egan went to bed early that night, wiped out by the day's frivolity, and Elaine and Owen cuddled up on the sofa, wine and music their only companions.

"Today was a wonderful surprise," Elaine said. "Thank you." She kissed him and ran her fingers over his light stubble.

"I know I work too much. I just want to give you everything you could ever want. I want the kids to have everything I didn't."

"What we want, Owen, is you."

"I know. Today reminded me of that. I'll cut back. Work regular hours. Or maybe work longer but take a day off each week?"

Elaine smiled, "We'll see." She knew Owen wanted to mean what he said, but his work always pulled him back in. She stood and held out a hand to him. He took it in his own and allowed his wife to lead him to the bedroom. With the children in deep sleep, the couple made love. They explored each other's bodies as if they had only just met and listened to the dawn chorus when they were finally spent, wrapped in each other's arms.

Egan screamed and spat his food out. Elaine sighed and wiped cauliflower from her eyebrow. "What *is* the matter with you, baby boy?"

"He's really grumpy today," Elaine's friend, Megan, said. She frowned and smiled at the infant in exaggerated moves, trying to make him laugh. Egan scowled in return.

"He's been grumpy for days. I don't know what's gotten into him."

"Is he sick?"

"I don't think so. His temperature is fine, he's eating well, when he isn't spitting it at me. He's..." she paused and eyed her friend before continuing. She smiled and screwed her face up before saying, "He smells different."

"What?" Megan laughed and tilted her head to appraise her friend.

"Egan smells different. I know it sounds weird, but he doesn't have that *Egan* smell anymore. He's usually so happy. It's like he's a completely different baby."

"What does Owen think?"

"He's just as grumpy," Elaine said, throwing her hands up in defeat as more food plastered her face and the walls. "A couple of weeks ago, he promised he would work less, but the very next day was out 'til gone midnight. We had a big fight because he'd promised to take Little Bug to dance class. She wanted to show him how she's getting on. She was so disappointed. Since then he's barely spoken to me."

"Men!"

"Tell me about it."

"Mummy." Little Bug entered the kitchen in a hurry, holding her cupped hands out to her mother. "I found a spider."

"Did you? Wow. Where was he?"

"In the bath. Can I take him outside?"

"Okay. You can play in the garden for a while if you'd like."

"Thank you."

Little Bug rushed to the back door and out into the garden. Elaine moved to the kitchen window to keep an eye on her.

"I thought I'd take Little Bug out at the weekend for ice-cream," Owen told Elaine that evening. The children were both in bed. Little Bug had fallen asleep with a book cradled in her arms and the silent baby monitor told them Egan was also in the land of nod. "Like we used to, just her and me."

"Like *we* used to," Elaine answered. She was more than a little irritated. When the children went to bed, Elaine and Owen finally had time to be a couple again. They would cuddle up on the sofa, drink wine, watch a movie or just talk about their day. On the rare occasions they weren't exhausted, they would even make love. That night, however, Owen had chosen to sit in the arm chair, away from Elaine. He had crossed his legs and turned on the television as if she wasn't waiting on the sofa, holding his wine out to him. Then he started talking about those days before Egan as though she hadn't been involved. "If you remember correctly, we *both* used to take *our* daughter for ice-cream. We would go as a family."

Owen frowned for a moment before saying, "Yes, I know, but you'll need to stay home with Egan." He smiled, a self-satisfied smirk on his face as if he'd talked his way out of that one.

"I don't see why Egan and I can't come along. Let's make it a family outing. We haven't done that in ages."

"We could, but then it wouldn't be a special treat for Bug."

"Why does she need a special treat? It's not her birthday, she's not upset or unhappy. And what about separating us makes it a special treat? She loves her little brother and she loves being all together."

Owen waved a dismissive hand at Elaine and looked back at the television. "Fine, fine. Was just an idea. Forget it."

"Forget it completely, or forget leaving out your wife and son?"

Owen stood abruptly and left the room saying, "Completely."

Elaine sighed and shook her head. What had just happened? What the hell was wrong with him? She sipped her wine, shaking her head once more.

"Bloody hell," Owen said. Elaine looked up, but he was not in the room. Her eyes moved to the baby monitor as Owen's voice said, "Idiot."

Was he referring to himself or to her? She realised she didn't really care. Pulling the blanket from the back of the sofa, she tucked her legs under her and watched the TV.

That Saturday, the family did indeed go for ice-cream. Egan frowned at the cold, soft substance they had put to his lips and refused to eat it.

"Egan," Elaine cajoled. "It's ice-cream. You love ice-cream."

"Not any more, apparently," Owen said.

"You're not eating it either," Elaine said. "What's the matter with you two lately?"

"What does that mean? Just because we don't want ice-cream there must be something wrong?"

"You're both as moody and temperamental as each other lately, that's what. It's driving me crazy. What is it? Bad time of the month?"

"Why does there have to be anything wrong? You're always looking for problems."

Elaine looked around her, seeing people trying not to watch their argument. She was embarrassed and tried to lighten her tone. "Why don't we go walk on the beach?"

The family moved to the shingle laden beach and watched the waves roll in and out as if the sea were a giant entity, breathing rhythmically. Little Bug chased the water as it receded before being chased back in again upon its return. Egan, who would normally laugh to see his sister running, simply watched with a detached stare.

"Do you think Egan's okay?" Elaine placed her palm on his forehead to feel for a temperature.

"Why?" Owen frowned at her as though she was crazy.

"He's not himself lately. I meant what I said, he's grumpy. He's usually such an easy going baby, but lately he's been off."

"Off? Don't be absurd. He's fine. You're worrying over nothing. Don't go all hysterical on me."

Elaine was shocked. Owen had never spoken to her like that and had always listened to her concerns about the children. She was good at spotting when they were off-colour and he knew to rely on that early warning system.

"Owen," she began, but stopped to compose herself. She wanted to sound rational and in control, something she felt he was accusing her of struggling to do. "Egan hasn't been himself for a few days now. He's not eating properly. He's fractious and unsettled. He frowns whenever Little Bug goes anywhere near him and he's difficult to settle at night."

"He was fine for me the other night," Owen said.

"Well, good for you, but he's being a brat for me."

"Don't call him that!" Owen was angry and Egan began to cry. Elaine couldn't understand the extreme reaction. She picked up Egan from his blanket on the stones and he screamed harder.

"Egan," she soothed. "Come on. Hush. Hush."

Egan continued to scream until Owen wrenched him from her arms, "Give him here." The baby stopped crying instantly.

"What's that all about?"

"You're upsetting him."

"How? He doesn't know what I'm saying. You scared him when you shouted."

"If he was so scared, why isn't he crying anymore? Huh?"

Elaine couldn't answer. She didn't know why. The whole thing was bizarre.

"Mummy," Little Bug called. "Mummy, come and play."

Before Elaine could answer her daughter, Owen stood with Egan and called, "We'll come and play, Bug. Mummy's not feeling well." He glared back at her as if daring her to disagree. She chose to sit in silence, frowning up at her husband and trying to figure out what had just happened.

Days later, things were still tense between husband and wife. Elaine had never experienced that side of Owen's personality and found herself wondering how she could have loved him for so long, lived with him for so many years without seeing the cold, vindictive man he could be. Egan continued to be difficult for her but angelic for Owen and her frustration grew. The final straw came when

Horror

she was alone with Little Bug one afternoon. She had put a restless Egan down for a nap, hoping sleep would temper his mood. Once the cries through the baby monitor had stopped, Little Bug had tugged on Elaine's sleeve. Bug had been subdued for a few days and Elaine had asked her what was wrong several times. She would always shake her head and say nothing.

"Mummy," Little Bug said in a tiny voice.

"Yes, my Little Bug."

"Can I tell you a secret?"

"You can tell me anything, baby."

Little Bug was silent for a few seconds, as if steeling herself to speak. Elaine began to worry about what her daughter might be about to say and was just about to speak when Little Bug said, "I don't like Daddy anymore." Her eyes were big and frightened, as if she was scared of her mother's response.

"Why?" Elaine felt the same way and had to be careful not to allow her own feelings to cloud her daughter's.

"He scares me, Mummy. I don't like it when he scares me."

"How does he scare you, baby?" Elaine felt a knot of sick worry balling in her gut. What had happened to make Bug so afraid of the one man who should make her feel safe? Elaine knew he wouldn't hurt their daughter, didn't she?

"He looks at me funny," Bug said in a whisper. She was looking at the floor, winding her finger into her skirt with nervous energy.

Elaine placed a finger under her daughter's chin and raised her face carefully to look her in the eyes. "Baby, tell me. Has Daddy done anything to hurt you?"

Little Bug shook her head, no.

"Has Daddy said anything to hurt you?"

Again she shook her head. Her curls swept across her face as she did so.

Elaine paused, thinking carefully. She didn't want to put words into Bug's mouth, but she needed to know. "Has Daddy said anything to scare you?"

Bug nodded her head, yes.

Elaine whispered now, "What?"

"He said…" Bug paused and then continued in a faltering whisper. "He said…I…I would be…with him…him and Egan…soon. He said, don't you want to come with us?"

Elaine couldn't understand what Bug was saying. The child continued with more strength in her voice. "He said we can all be together."

"Why is that scary, Bug? Don't you want to be all together?"

"He had scary eyes, Mummy. Scary, scary eyes. I didn't like it."

"I'm sure Daddy didn't mean to scare you, baby."

"He looks at me funny. So does Egan."

"Egan's just a baby, Bug. He can't do anything. He's just been a bit grumpy lately. I think he's coming down with something. That's all."

Little Bug dropped her eyes to the floor once more. She whispered, "Okay, Mummy," and tried to leave. Elaine held onto her arm and pulled her into a hug. She whispered into her daughter's hair that she loved her and Daddy loved her and Egan loved her. She held her until she felt the soft shudders of crying begin and she held her until those shudders subsided. Eventually Little Bug pulled away and Elaine let her go. "He's not Daddy, not really," she said and left the room.

Later that night Elaine talked to Owen about his change in mood.

"I don't know what's changed, Owen." Elaine kept her voice soft as she tried to avoid accusation creeping into her words.

"Nothing's changed," Owen answered. He looked at the floor, a hang nail, his phone, anything to avoid looking at his wife. She pressed on.

"I can't help you if I don't know what's wrong. I can't put it right if it's me that's the problem."

She paused, giving him space to answer but he did not.

"Owen, please?"

"What do you want me to say?" He glared at her, eyes blazing. "Everything's fine. Bloody hell!"

"That's what I'm talking about," she said, finally allowing the irritation to show. "You're moody, defensive and aggressive. Even Bug is afraid of you." She hadn't meant to tell him that. No matter how bad his behaviour, she knew he would be hurt by that knowledge and he didn't deserve that.

Owen shot to his feet, fists clenched and face white. "Bug? Scared of me? Ludicrous."

"I'm sorry, Owen. I didn't want to tell you that. She's only little. She misreads things and thinks it's all her fault. She thinks you're angry at her rather than simply angry."

"What the hell is that supposed to mean?"

"You're angry, Owen. Look at yourself. You're angry all the time. Children pick up on these things. Egan's noticed it too. He's been restless and grouchy almost as long as you have. Little Bug isn't used to seeing you angry. It scares her."

With his fist raised to the ceiling, towards the room where Little Bug slept, Owen shouted, "Scared? I'll give the little bitch something to be scared about!"

Horror

Elaine shot up from her seat and barred the door before Owen could leave the room and head upstairs. "Get out of this house, Owen," she demanded. "You stay away from our daughter and you get the hell out of this house."

A menacing gleam lit Owen's eyes as he sneered and said in a low growl, "You going to kick me out? I'd love to see you try."

Elaine's husband, her companion, the love of her life was gone. In his place was a man she didn't know, didn't want to know and was just as afraid of as her daughter was. She had to get the children out of the house. She had to get them safely away.

"Move, bitch."

"Get out of this house, Owen. I will not let you near our children until you've calmed down."

He grabbed her arms in his large, strong hands and pulled her into the room, casually throwing her to one side as he did so. With his egress free, he stormed out and ran up the stairs. "Little Bug, Little Bug, let me come in," he said in a wolf-like voice, turning one of her favourite nursery rhymes into a terrifying hunter's cry.

"No!"

Elaine raced after him, grabbing at his clothes, trying to stop him. He shoved his elbow back and pain burst through her ribs from the impact. She lost her balance and fell backwards, down the stairs. With a hard slam to the back of her head, she landed at the bottom and was momentarily stunned into immobility. The world turned to black before returning as a blur of noise and light. Egan's high-pitched wails pierced the cloak of fog and brought her some way back to her senses.

"Little Bug," Owen called.

"No," Elaine said, shocked by the weakness of her voice. She pushed herself up off the floor and climbed the stairs on her hands and knees. Nausea washed over in waves and she fought it down as she slowly clambered up the stairs.

"Little Bug."

His taunting calls terrified her. She had never imagined he could be so cruel. He wasn't her Owen – something had changed him. As she reached the top step, Owen's boots met her. She looked up at him, struggling against vertigo as she did so.

"What have you done with her?"

Little Bug must be hiding. Good girl. "I put her to bed…as usual," she managed to say. He stepped over her and stomped down the stairs. Unable to stand listening to Egan's cries any longer, Elaine struggled to her feet and stumbled into the nursery. Egan stood in his cot, red faced and furious. She rushed over and picked him up. She held him close, cooing and soothing as best she could. She whispered, "Little Bug, where are you, baby?"

From behind a chest of drawers inside the open wardrobe, a little face peered out. Elaine's little girl was terrified. Her pale face and wide eyes glowed in the dark at the back of the wardrobe. "Come here, baby." She bent down and held one arm out to her daughter while cradling her son with the other.

Egan screamed louder as Little Bug crept to her mother's side. She did not cry. She simply stared her gaping eyes up at Elaine in shock and fear. "Where's Daddy?" Her voice was tiny, almost inaudible.

"Oh my baby," Elaine said, tears flowing freely down her face. "My poor baby. Don't you worry. Mummy will keep you safe. Hush, Egan. Hush now."

Elaine stood. She gripped tightly to Egan and Little Bug as she crept out of the nursery. A bang shot through the house, reverberating around the walls. All three jumped at the sound and Elaine froze and waited in the silence that followed. When the silence dragged on, Elaine assumed Owen had stormed out of the house, slamming the door behind him. With careful, deliberate movements, Elaine and Little Bug moved down the stairs. The slamming of the door had shocked Egan into silence and Elaine was grateful for it. They reached the ground floor and Elaine rushed to the front door.

The frame was twisted and the door pulled halfway through to the other side. It must have been slammed with incredible force to pull it through the frame. It could not be moved. Elaine turned and made her way down the hall to the back of the house, intending to leave by the back door. Little Bug moved in stiff jerks at her side, clinging with a desperate grip onto her leg. They froze as one when the back door banged open. Elaine was trapped. The front door was stuck and Owen was at the back. Little Bug pulled on her jeans and pointed to the door under the stairs.

"Yes," Elaine whispered. "Good girl."

They opened the door and crept inside. Elaine was expecting to huddle in the confined space of the little triangular cupboard. Instead, a ladder descended from a hole in the floor, hidden from view by a box that was laid over the top. When Elaine had moved it to give them room, she found the hole. "Climb down, baby."

To Elaine's surprise, Little Bug did as she was told, not complaining about the dark, the ladder or the cold of the cellar beneath. The fear of her father far outweighed the fear of this new situation. Elaine waited until Little Bug reached the bottom and then followed with care, only one hand available to hold the rungs as she clutched her baby to her breast.

Horror

"Move away from the ladder, baby. We need to hide."

Elaine led her daughter to the darkest corner of the cellar and hunkered down amongst some old newspapers, piles of blankets, pillows and cushions. It gave a soft place to lay Egan while Elaine caught her breath and flexed her aching arm. Little Bug climbed onto her lap and she stroked the child's hair as she tried to make sense of everything. She stopped stroking when Little Bug froze once more. "What is it baby?"

Little Bug wouldn't speak. She simply pointed to something buried beneath the cushions. Elaine squinted in an effort to see what the pale, spiked object was. She moved her daughter off her lap and leaned closer to examine it. Moving the pillow that obscured it, she revealed a pale, waxy hand. It looked like that of a mannequin, except for the detail of the nails, the creases in the knuckles and the platinum wedding band on the ring finger. Elaine's breath caught as she stared at the hand. It was the hand that she was used to holding, the fingers that caressed her body and tickled Little Bug and Egan. It was Owen's hand.

Elaine pulled at the cushions and blankets, revealing her husband's body, cold and lifeless with blank, staring eyes. A gaping red gash stretched across his throat. Blood covered neck and clothes but none was spilled onto the floor or bedding around him. She couldn't believe what she was seeing. Her husband was upstairs, hunting them. Her husband was lying dead in their cellar. How was that possible? Her eyes burned and filled with tears. Her beautiful Owen was gone.

"What is it, Mummy?" Little Bug was shielded from the gruesome find by Elaine's body, but the girl's voice brought her back to the moment. Her priority was keeping her children safe. Whatever was masquerading as her husband was a threat to their safety. She could mourn her husband, and figure out what the hell was happening, once the children were safe. She covered Owen once more, to protect the children from seeing his body. Little Bug was rocking gently, holding her knees in front of her and staring at something only she could see. Egan was watching Elaine. His eyes showed an intelligence and awareness that seemed far beyond his years. He looked down at the covered body of his father and then back to her. Had he seen?

"Egan?" Elaine reached over to him, but his face changed to a grimace and he pushed her hand away. "Egan, baby. What's the matter?"

"He's scary, like Daddy," Little Bug said. Her voice was hollow and void of any intonation, just a certainty that chilled Elaine's heart.

"What do you mean, baby?"

"Daddy's scary. Egan's scary too," Little Bug answered in the same empty, emotionless voice.

Elaine began frantically pulling up cushions, pillows, papers and blankets until she found a chubby little leg, as cold and lifeless as Owen had been. She reached into the pile and pulled the body of her baby into her arms. The fake Egan shrieked and laughed at her. His baby movements, usually so cute in their honesty and innocence, were cold, threatening and evil. Elaine held her baby's body and wept. She could feel the sticky blood that covered him. She couldn't bear to see the wound she knew would bisect his throat. Little Bug began to cry as she too realised her brother was dead and an imposter hid with them in the cellar. She hugged close to Elaine who pulled her out from their hiding place in an effort to get away from the demonic baby.

"Daddy's here!"

Elaine spun round and Little Bug shrieked. The fake Owen stood at the bottom of the stairs, smiling. She struggled to speak, "What are you?"

"Not necessary to explain, my dear. It's your turn now. I've been trying to get time alone with the Bug girl for weeks, but you never seem to let her out of your sight."

Elaine pulled Little Bug round behind her legs, shielding her from the man they had thought loved them. "Owen," Elaine began, but then stopped. Not Owen. "Why? How?"

The fake Owen sneered and Elaine shook her head. This couldn't be happening. This had to be some kind of sick joke. "Owen, how could you do this? I loved you. I trusted you."

"You trusted him," the fake Owen said, tilting his head towards where Owen's body lay.

"No. I trusted *you*. You were there. You were my husband. You were Egan and Little Bug's father." Elaine stroked Little Bug's hair and kissed her forehead, but never once stopped watching the fake Owen. Little Bug shivered in her arms. "You were our family and we trusted you."

He shrugged, nonchalant and unmoved by her words. "Look, I'm not going to stand here and chat all day." He clapped his hands in two, sharp cracks as if he were calling a waiter in a restaurant. "Time to go now. We thank you for your contribution."

"Our what?" Before Elaine could say more, two figures began to descend the steps to the cellar. One was a slim redhead holding the hand of a small girl with ringlets in her hair. Elaine and Little Bug, or facsimiles of them, smiled as they reached the cellar floor.

Horror

"It won't take long," the fake Owen said. "Don't fight. It just makes it harder."

Elaine crumpled to the floor and held tightly to her daughter. "I'm sorry, baby. I'm so sorry." The doppelgangers closed in.

The End

T.D. Harvey has been writing stories since she first put pen to paper. Even though she has lived in Philadelphia in the USA, Caerleon in Wales and Bristol in England, she always returns home to Hampshire, England and sets much of her writing in that beautiful and historic county. In her previous career as a qualified Veterinary Nurse, her writing often revolved around animal stories and thrillers based in the veterinary world. Today, she sees herself more as a dark fiction author for children and adults. Although her writing spans many genres, it always errs on the darker side.

She juggles her writing with a full-time Business Analyst career, looking after her two Tonkinese cats, her Fahaka puffer fish and assorted other freshwater fish, growing her own fruit and vegetables and managing her chronic pain condition, Fibromyalgia. Ms. Harvey has been published in several anthologies including, *Flash It!*, *Anything Goes* and *Writers' Anarchy III: Heroes and Villains*. Ms. Harvey plans to publish her debut novel, *Paper Dragons and Shadow Demons*, a middle grade, dark fiction/fantasy story about the things all children fear, in 2016.

Find her on:

Website: http://tdharveyauthor.wordpress.com/

Facebook: https://www.facebook.com/T.D.HarveyAuthor

A Note

Raitt Black

Life is a continuous journey of learning and growth, even until the finality of death. Music called Shane along his path and he walked it with a guitar strapped to the pack on his back, until the day he stood at the junction road to Reyem, map in hand, weighing the risks. The city was considered a haven for thieves and mercenaries. He had been urged to avoid it, but Shane knew from experience: sometimes musicians thrived where all else was dim.

A gust of wind plucked the map from his hands and blew it into the woods. He chased the fluttering paper until it stuck in a tree branch, rustling against the wind. When he grabbed it, he noticed a path leading into the woods. It was overgrown with brambles and saplings, but he was certain it was there. A sign lay on the ground beside the path, weathered and off its base, leaning against a tree. The grooves of the carved lettering had worn smooth around the edges, and where the sign rested along the ground, it had rotted and fallen away but enough remained to read a name.

Hyerton. And beside it, the number eighty-four.

He checked his map, found Reyem, and traced the line of the road to his location. Nothing on the map indicated anything noteworthy at the junction, nor around it. Thinking about it, he had never heard mention of the town before, and he could not recall ever meeting anyone from Hyerton.

The mystery of a secret town intrigued him, but he eyed the wooden sign with distrust. He studied every musician he met. Learned their phrases, melodies, and flow. As a traveling musician he eagerly played along with any style he heard, and earned his living singing and playing for every audience he found, but each musician he met was at least from *somewhere*.

The late afternoon sun and looming darkness reminded him he needed shelter for the night. He glanced about. The trees looked oddly thick here, their limbs and branches like spindly arms and claws. These woods were not an inviting

Horror

forest to sleep in. He shuddered and hoped to find shelter in Hyerton. Even if the town was abandoned, he preferred to sleep in anything man-made.

Shane battled the thorns and thick vines of overgrowth, wondering if it was worth it, but persisted and broke through. He stopped before rounding a hill and looked back. Through the fading light of the day he saw the road and junction sitting on the horizon, almost within reach. He knew he could turn back, continue along the road until he found a clearing and camp there for the night, but the temptation of Hyerton persisted. An unknown town might mean new music. The thought called to him, and he followed the path further into the woods. When the trees thinned around a bend and the forest opened into a clearing, he noticed buildings and stopped. Shane hid behind a tree and watched the town for signs of life.

The black soil of the clearing, freshly tilled and ready for planting, was separated into square patches by smoothed, foot-worn paths. The single dirt road was bracketed on either side by small wooden buildings so close together, it was difficult to see where each began and ended. Only one was tall enough to have a second floor, and he guessed it was a tavern. A sign, which hung from the upper facade, jutted out above the dirt street.

The door opened, spilling light onto the twilight shaded dirt road, and a man wearing dark overalls and a wide-brimmed hat emerged.

Shane leaned against the tree and watched. The lone man walked away along the road. His presence accentuated the discord of the tightly packed town and well-divided field. Shane took quick stock of the field, counting the squares at twelve on the long edge and seven on the short edge. With a little effort, he added twelve to itself seven times and came up with eighty-four.

"The number on the sign," he muttered and counted it out again to be sure.

The man in the road entered a building near the outskirts of town. Shane waited for the door to close before approaching the town himself. He pushed against the tree and his fingers slipped into a knothole. Sap clung to his fingers when he pulled his hand away. Grimacing, he wiped it on the tree bark and looked at the knothole. It was shaped like an ear without a lobe.

"Looks like I don't have to sleep under you tonight," Shane said to the tree.

Knowing he would be easy to see against the empty fields surrounding the town, Shane thought of it as a stage and strolled with cheerful confidence to hide his unease. He went to the only lit building, the yellow-hued glow of kerosene lamps spilled far enough into the road to light the sign, *Hyerton*. Below that, the number eighty-four. He swallowed, wondered about the significance of the number, and went inside.

All eyes turned to him as he stopped, unsure which way to go. The handful of patrons turned their unkempt beards and weathered hats of various sun-bleached shades and stared at him. He walked to the bar, careful not to meet anyone's gaze, and sat on a stool.

The bartender broke the silence. "Drink?" Her pregnant belly looked ready to push a new life into the world at any moment.

"Please," Shane said.

She eyed a man in black overalls seated at a nearby table. "We'll need two, now."

"Yes we will," he answered. One of his eyes was clouded over with blindness.

"Money?" the barkeep asked.

"None," Shane answered. "I have none, but I do have a guitar. I can sing a song or two in exchange for food and drink."

She glared at him.

Shane looked from her to a tavern patron and wondered if they spoke the same language. Then the barkeep laughed. The quick bark of a laugh brought smiles to the patrons' faces and soon they all joined the raucous.

"Go on. Stage is there." The barkeep pointed toward the opposite wall. "Play some, then eat. There's a seat for every butt."

Shane nodded and went to the stage. He set his pack down, brought his guitar out of its case, and sat on the only stool on stage. "I just need a moment to tune." He plucked the A string on his guitar. The general conversations in the room stopped and everyone hummed the note. He stopped tuning and glanced about. "I..." he went silent when he realized everyone was staring at him. The intent gaze in their eyes was familiar, but Shane could not recall from where. Their humming softened as the note from his guitar faded. "I can't tune if you hum along."

"Just play," the barkeep called across the tavern.

So he played a simple instrumental, enough to determine his guitar was still in tune. Then he started a workman's song.

"Shut it!" a thin man in black overalls yelled.

"No work!" another called.

"The Old Country!" the man in black overalls yelled. He raised his mug and stood as the others called "The Old Country" back to him, then they all drank what remained in their mugs.

It had been a long time since Shane met such an agreeable bunch, and it relaxed him. After a song of the Old Country he transitioned to a love song. The tavern patrons welcomed it with cheers and sang along, somehow having heard it before. Halfway through, the tavern door swung open.

Horror

Shane played a few more notes, until he recognized what the new patron carried. It was a guitar case. The man walked toward the stage, the fall of each boot heal echoing across the now silent tavern. His long gray hair swayed as he walked.

"Kyle, we didn't know you'd be here tonight," the half blind man in black overalls said, his head downcast and shoulders slumped in deference to Kyle.

Without breaking his stride, Kyle looked at the overalled man, raised his index finger to his lips to shush him, and continued onto the stage. The stubble of Kyle's beard matched the gray of his hair but for one odd patch of black, off-center on the side of his chin. He stopped in front of Shane and said, "You're in my spot," in a quiet, matter-of-fact tone.

"My pardon, sir," Shane said. "I didn't know it was yours." He thought the audience would laugh at his witticism. Instead, they remained deathly silent. A moment later he stood and moved away from the stool.

"The stage is my spot," Kyle said.

Shane looked at Kyle, the audience, the barkeep, and back to Kyle. "Does anybody else play here?"

"Let him play," a new voice shouted from the audience. Then another voice shouted agreement. Soon there was a general clamoring for the music to continue.

Kyle set his guitar case down on the stage with a slow reverence, and turned to the tavern patrons. He raised his arms, outstretched on either side, with his hands open and facing the audience, like a pastor calming his flock. They quieted to silence a moment later.

In a hushed voice, Kyle spoke to the crowd, "You know the rules, yet you let him play."

Shane was amazed the audience could hear Kyle; he spoke in a near whisper.

Kyle faced Shane and asked, "What's your name?"

"Shane."

"Now Shane," Kyle said, "to play on my stage, in my tavern, in my town, you must earn the right. You must choose a song. It can be any song but you must write it or choose it, no one can choose it for you. We will each play one song. The audience will choose the winner. Only if you win will you be allowed again on my stage." Kyle stopped.

The pause allowed the rules a moment of clarity in Shane's mind. One song each, chosen by the performer, winner decided by the crowd. It was straightforward enough. Shane nodded his agreement.

"The townspeople will gather tonight to hear us play. In the meantime, you will be fed and given a room upstairs to rest. Choose your song wisely or leave. It matters not to me."

"What happens if I don't win?"

"It's a song." Kyle shrugged. "If you don't win, you don't play again on my stage."

Shane nodded. The contest was simple enough. "Thank you for the room and meal."

Kyle picked up his guitar case and turned to the audience. "Gather Hyerton, we have business to tend." He walked off the stage. The murmurs of the audience did not stop him, nor hinder his already slow pace as he walked to the door and out of the tavern. Most of the patrons followed suit, except for a few men in black overalls. The man with the blinded eye was one of them, and he sat staring at the door.

The barkeep approached the stage. "I'll show you the room. Leave your pack stuff there and come back down for food."

"Is this normal?" Shane asked. "I don't mean to sound ungrateful, but I've never had anything like this happen before. Most musicians like to play with others."

"It's normal," she said. "Kyle is protective of Hyerton. He grew up here, doesn't want to see it change. Pack your guitar, I'll show you upstairs."

Shane packed his guitar and followed the barkeep upstairs to the room. It was small and plain with a simple nightstand beside the bed and a single window. A patch of wallpaper was missing from the wall, which revealed the dark wood beneath. He placed his guitar and pack in a corner of the room and sat on the bed. He tried to think which song to play, but there were too many to choose from. Tales of battles and the creation of kingdoms. Of lovers lost to the infatuation of each other. The virtuous and the wicked and how sometimes they could be one and the same. His stomach grumbled and complained of emptiness, so Shane went downstairs.

The barkeep brought him a bowl of potato soup, then leaned back and rubbed her pregnant belly. "So what song will you play?"

"I don't know," Shane replied. "There are so many to choose from, and I don't know anything about Hyerton."

"I'll give you a hint." The barkeep winced and rubbed a different spot on her belly. "Sorry, baby likes to kick. Listen, Hyerton's a small town. The judges are all the folks that can fit in here. Sing about them. Sing about the town they call home. It's the only way to win them over."

Shane thought about it and realized her insight made sense. What better song could there be than one about the people he needed to impress? He thanked her and glanced about the tavern. Only a few men remained. Feeling his belly grumble again, Shane decided to eat first.

A hand rested on his shoulder and gripped him, firmer than any in his memory.

Horror

Shane turned and faced a man in black overalls, his one good eye staring back at him.

"Come on." The man pulled Shane up from the seat and led him to a table. "I'm Delik," he said. "You want to stay away from the older folks in Hyerton. They all had the bumps. It makes them crazy when they get old. Right boys?"

The five men at the table nodded. Any one of them was easily bigger than Delik, but they quietly deferred to the half blind man.

"You need a song, right?"

Shane nodded.

"We're the men to talk to."

The others nodded. They all wore black overalls, as if they were in uniforms.

"We're the Hyerton Scalpers. Anybody starts trouble around here, we settle it. So we know about everything that happens in Hyerton. Get it?"

Shane nodded and looked at each of the Scalpers. None of them alone looked like they could tell a story or remember a detail enough to earn a free meal, never mind help write or choose a song for a contest. But they were the only other patrons in the tavern, and Shane didn't think he had much of a choice. "Anybody ever kill anyone around here?"

The Scalpers stared at Shane until Delik broke the silence. He leaned close. His blinded eye, clouded and misshapen, moved in unison with his good eye. He said, "Only people ever get killed in these parts are traveling sing-songers." Delik smacked Shane's back and roared into laughter, followed by the other Scalpers.

"We're just joking on you," one of them said between laughs, but Shane wondered again why he'd never heard of Hyerton.

"Come on, drink up lad," Delik said. "Listen and learn. We'll tell you all you need for that song of yours." He raised his mug and the others joined him.

Shane pushed his unease aside and joined the Scalpers in their merriment. They made quick work of the drinks and emptied the mugs.

An older, gray haired Scalper spoke, his voice a smooth, serene calm. "Hyerton only been here a few hundred years. Most maps don't see us, and we like to keep it that way. Hyerton takes care of herself. Our plots yield plenty of crops for everybody here. There's fresh water from the mountains. People are good, hard working folk and take care of their own. We all know to stay out of the woods after dark. Nobody wants to see the things out there."

"What things?" Shane asked.

"We don't know what they are, or where they came from, but they've been out there for as long as Hyerton been around. Every time a new person comes to town, they come alive and hunt us. We don't know why, but they only let eighty-four of us live here. So whenever a traveler comes to town, or a baby is born, we give a sacrifice to keep the town safe." The gray haired Scalper stared at Shane.

"Eighty four? The number on the sign?"

Old gray nodded.

"Why don't you leave?" Shane asked. He glanced at the other Scalpers and noticed all the others were younger, with dark chestnut and black hair.

"We can't," the old gray haired Scalper answered, "because it's a good story and scared you." The Scalpers smiled and laughed at Shane's worried expression, until Delik calmed them.

"Shane, there's not much special about Hyerton. We grow crops. We hunt in the woods. We make young'uns to carry on after we're gone. We don't want to be on your map, so we don't trade with outsiders. It's a simple life, well-lived. What more could anyone want?" Delik leaned back in his chair, stretched his arms, and rested his hands behind his head. The grin on his face spoke both of years of hard work and the satisfaction of the results, despite the blinded eye.

Shane wondered why he had been worried.

"If you want," the gray haired Scalper said, "the best song we can hear is about the best life there is. All about the earth giving back to the work put into it, the love of a good mate, and the joy of healthy children."

Surprised, Shane gaped at how easy the old man made it sound. "That's all?"

Old gray nodded.

"A song about the rewards of living off the land?"

"Aye," Delik confirmed.

"A drink to the land," old gray hair suggested. They went to the bar for another mug each, toasted the land, and drank.

"I should go pick a song," Shane said, eager to leave before he achieved inebriation.

"To the room," Delik commanded. "I'll get you when the time comes."

Shane agreed and went to his room. He sat and played through a few songs, but none struck him as noteworthy. There was something lacking in each of them, though they were otherwise good. He decided to check his songbook and perhaps find one he was overlooking in his memory. But after a cursory glance around the room, he did not see his pack. He checked under the bed and nightstand, but it was not in the room. Dumbfounded, Shane checked again. There were limited hiding spots, and his search lasted only a few moments. His pack was gone. He went to the door and opened it. A Scalper sat like a watchman on a stool in the hall.

"Get back in there," the Scalper said. "It's not time for sing-songing."

Horror

"My pack is gone."

"You'll get it back if you win tonight."

Shane stared at the Scalper, unsure if he had heard him correctly. "I was told it would be safe in the room."

"Were you now?"

Shane considered the question and could not recall with certainty. "I need my pack."

"Win tonight."

Shane leaned toward the stairs and called out, "Delik."

The Scalper stood. "Delik don't have it. Get back in the room."

Shane called out again. The Scalper grabbed him by the shoulders and shoved him back into the room.

"Choose your song." The Scalper slammed the door and locked it.

The dead click of the lock reverberated through the door. Shane realized he was trapped in Hyerton to play a song for these people, and the only prize was being allowed to play on Kyle's stage. He had asked what would happen if he lost and was given a simple answer. Kyle had said, "If you don't win, you don't play again on my stage." None of that sounded like a threat, but the Scalper would not let him leave.

He leaped toward the door and pounded on it.

"Let me out."

"Pick your song."

Shane yelled again for freedom and the Scalper ignored him, so Shane asked, "What happens if I lose?"

There was no answer.

"What happens if I lose?" Shane yelled.

"Quit your carrying on." The Scalper's voice was muffled through the door. "It's a song, we just don't want you to leave."

Shane pounded on the door and yelled until his knuckles bled and his voice hurt. Only silence answered. He turned and leaned his back against the door, and saw the window across the room.

He rushed to it and tried to open it, but the window would not budge. He felt around for a lock and found none. The glass was one solid piece and the wooden-cross facade merely created the appearance of four panes of glass. It would only open if broken. He went to the nightstand and tried to lift it, to break the window and escape, but it was nailed to the floor. So was the bed.

For a moment he thought to use his guitar, but the hollow acoustic instrument would likely break against the crossbeams. Besides, there was no guarantee Kyle would share his guitar if Shane's was suddenly unplayable. The only way out of the room was through the locked door.

Shane knew he had to pick a song to play. His mind raced through songs he knew and settled on one called "The Anum." It was a traditional tune and would fit well enough in the situation.

He grabbed his guitar. His fingers shook and he missed what would otherwise be simple movements, but eventually he plucked out the root notes of the tune. He paused, calmed himself, and continued until he elaborated to the chord progression. The interplay of the tune and the chords was masterfully simplistic. He rehearsed the lyrics with the melody and chord progressions, singing of a crisp spring morning and the farmer who greeted it, thankful for the recent thaw. He sang of the plowing and planting and the family that helped through it all. Of how summers pass with chores to be done and children underfoot. The simple pleasure of a cool breeze on a midsummer afternoon, and the infectious joy of the laughter of youth. He continued into the toils of the harvest, preparations for winter, and finished with the All Souls festival to remember the generations before. A reminder they continued to watch and protect all.

To finish, he sang a softer stanza about winter. The dormant, restful season which completes the circle into spring. The seasons move on, as do we all.

He finished singing and held the last note on the guitar. The open G chord hovered in the room as the reverberation of the guitar ebbed and slowed to silence. Calmed after a pass through the song, he thought it would be enough to impress the crowd. Not knowing when Delik would come, he wanted to rehearse the song a few times, but was distracted by a tapping at the window.

It repeated upon the glass, a chaotic rhythm that bore into his head. Wind came and went, but the tapping continued unaffected. Unable to concentrate, he leaned back toward the window.

The noise stopped.

Peering out into the moon-thinned darkness, he saw a tree branch. Though the tip was only a few feet from the glass, it did not look close enough to tap on it. Perhaps, if someone climbed the tree they could push the branch and smack it against the window, but there was no sign of anyone outside. Not on the ground or in the tree.

He watched the tree, waited for a breeze or an animal to sway it, but nothing did. The only oddity he noticed was a knothole below the lowest branches with an oval like an ear missing its lobe, much like the one in the tree at the edge of the field. A coincidence, he told himself, and went to practice the song.

The door unlocked, alerting him it was time. Delik and the old gray haired

Horror

Scalper entered and shut the door behind them.

"Shane," Delik said. He paused and ran his fingers through his thick black hair, letting it fall to cover his bad eye. "We need your help."

"What do you mean?" Shane tensed.

"Kyle's never lost," Delik said, "but he needs to tonight."

"Kyle blinded Delik's eye," old gray haired said. "Held a hot fire poker up close enough to ruin his sight."

"Why?"

"Because I said he should be next," Delik answered.

Shane looked from Delik to old gray. "Next for what?"

"The monsters are real," old gray hair said.

Shane stared at them. "Is this a joke?"

"No," Delik said. "We want you to win tonight."

"So we brought you Kyle's song. It wins every time." Old gray hair held out a piece of paper. "All we know is you play the one note over and over again. When you tuned yesterday, and everyone looked at you and you stopped. That's the note."

"The A?"

They nodded. "Kyle called it a chord, once," old gray hair said. "He won't let nobody else touch his guitar. We can't figure out how to play it."

Shane took the paper and scanned the lyrics.

"Kyle wins with this song every time," Delik said.

The words were simple. An ode to the land and the kinship of the townspeople, but quickly turned dark. Shane's hands shook as he read the last stanza. "I can't sing this."

"You have to, or Kyle wins," Delik said.

Sensing this would be his last chance to bow out, Shane said, "I want to go home."

"It's too late now. The things in the woods want a sacrifice. They only let eighty-four of us live, and when you came to Hyerton that makes one too many. The song is your choice." Delik grasped him by the shoulder. "But I hope it's the right one."

"Kyle said I could leave, it makes no difference to him."

"He did, but he'll sing the song as you go. Even if he didn't sing, the things in the woods will get you."

"The monsters?" Shane asked.

"Aye," both Delik and old gray hair said.

Old gray offered one last bit of advice. "Just don't stop. Whatever happens, play the song all the way through to the end."

Shane wanted to run, but knew of no way out. The only exit was through the tavern.

"Better learn those words. We'll give you a moment."

Shane watched them leave, trying to guess if this was another joke, but fearing it was not. Frantic, he memorized the lyrics and practiced the short song until the door opened and Delik beckoned for him to follow.

They walked to the stairs and Shane saw the tavern was full. Every chair at every table, each of the barstools, all were occupied. People stood in the aisles and walkways and leaned against walls. Children sat on tables, crowded together so they would not fall off. It looked impossible to walk to the stage, the only spot with any open space. Only Kyle, his guitar case, and two stools occupied the stage.

Shaking, he nearly fell down the stairs and managed to scrape his guitar strings on the railing. The sound mimicked the sinking feeling he felt inside.

"Clear a path!" Delik bellowed and motioned for Shane to follow him. They shuffled through the crowd with barely room to avoid bumping shoulders with the audience or step on their toes. Whispers and hushed comments too soft to discern were the only other sounds in the room. Once onstage, he turned to the crowd.

"Is he big enough?" a woman in the back of the audience called, which was followed by a few laughs from the crowd.

"He'll be fine," Delik said, loud enough for all to hear.

"What did she mean by that?" Shane asked.

"She wanted to know if they'd all hear you," Kyle stated. His guitar was still in its case. An old, faded black case with white stitching. Battered and dented, the finish had peeled along an edge and revealed the light wood grain beneath. He leaned down and opened the case. The guitar he took out had cracks in the finish. Only the four middle strings were attached, the low E string was completely gone and the high E string hung from the tuning peg on the headstock. A few of the frets had fallen off the fret board, leaving slivers of emptiness in the rosewood fingerboard.

Shane wondered if the guitar was playable.

Kyle rested the guitar on his thigh and plucked each of the four strings. The guitar was in tune, much to Shane's surprise. The crowd in the tavern waited for Kyle to begin his song. He plucked the A string and let the note resound.

Delik interrupted. He stepped up and addressed the audience with a quick introduction. "You all know Kyle. So tonight, we first give the stage to the newcomer. Shane." He raised his hands in applause until everyone clapped, then bowed to Shane and in a few brisk steps stood next to Kyle.

Horror

Shane plucked the A string on his guitar, thankful it was still in tune despite scraping the stair railing. He noticed a few patrons in front, near the stage, tilted their heads and had an odd look in their eyes, as if the note itself affected them. Odd though it was, he ignored it. The audience had almost finished their applause and he had to begin.

For a moment he faltered and could not decide which song to play while the eager crowd waited. He turned and looked at Kyle. The old musician stared back.

Shane turned to the audience and plucked the A note. A chorus of tones all hummed the one note along with the guitar, and a few people looked more intent and focused as they stared at the stage.

He formed an A chord and plucked all four strings. The crowd hummed the notes in a perfect, mimicked echo of the chord. The men hummed the low note, women hummed the middle two notes, and the children hummed the higher note. A few more people gained an eerie intensity to their gazes.

"No," Kyle protested, but Delik grabbed his shoulder and forced him to remain seated.

Keeping the dark references of the song lyrics in mind, Shane switched his fingers to an A-minor chord and strummed it to life with a swift down stroke. A few people shifted in their chairs as the sound echoed in the room, made louder by the voices of the audience humming along. Every patron focused on the stage, but it was a child that reminded Shane where he had seen the look before. A child who shifted into a crouch on a table and looked ready to pounce like a cat fixated on a mouse. Even though it was Shane who played the notes, every predatory gaze from the audience was directed at Kyle.

Shane sang the song Delik had given him.

"These are my kin,
this is my home,
I am from here,
and not alone."

At the end of each line Shane strummed the guitar again, and with each stroke the crowd hummed on beat.

"That's my song," Kyle protested.

Shane continued.

"We know the land,
we breathe the air,
and for your life,
we thank you fair."

"You can't play that." Kyle pushed against Delik, but the one-eyed Scalper held firm.

Shane paused. The next lyrics escaped him for a moment, but he remembered and continued.

"Don't matter how,
or what you say,
nor what you sing,
or what you play."

A child on a tabletop gnashed his teeth and looked ready to leap to the stage. The people seated closest to Shane stood and moved to the edge of the stage, hunched like predators on the hunt. As the song continued, other people moved forward to fill the space. Shane backed a step away from the crowd. He looked at Delik. The Scalper nodded and held Kyle. The old musician struggled to free himself but merely flailed against Delik's grip. Shane continued.

"Your flesh will grow,
our crops from dirt,
and spirit roam,
our sacred earth."

"This isn't funny!" Kyle protested.

But Shane understood it was no joke. There was a reason why no traveling musicians came from Hyerton. He continued.

"Come one and all,
don't wait too long,
reap his blood,
I'll sing along."

While Shane sang the last stanza, the audience advanced onto the stage, children leaped and clawed over the backs of the adults. Kyle screamed and was subdued in moments. Despite his thrashing and pleading, the crowd lifted and carried him through the tavern.

Only a few people could fit through the doorway at a time, and the Scalpers took the burden from the crowd. Kyle struggled harder against them but only managed to swing his head from side to side, his arms and legs would not budge from their grips. The men in black overalls carried him across the road and into the field. Delik gripped Shane's arm and they followed the crowd.

"Let me go," Kyle screamed.

"Hum the note and don't stop," Delik whispered to Shane. "It approaches your plot."

"My plot?" Shane squinted to see what Delik spoke of, but only saw the people from the tavern. They stopped at the edge of the road, refusing to enter

Horror

the field. Their voices were still humming and singing. A monstrous bellowing mimicked the A note.

"Your land," Delik said. "Your sacred earth, your square of the field. Hum the note you played and only stop to breathe."

"Why?" Shane asked.

Delik slipped through the crowd, pulling Shane along with him, and pointed at a tree in the middle of the clearing. Shane was certain it had not been there when he arrived in Hyerton.

"The tree will sacrifice Kyle to the land, to help grow your crops this summer."

The bellowing sound stopped. The tree's branches shook and rustled its small, green spring leaves. Then the bellowing continued, as if it had paused to breathe.

The tree took a step.

Roots pulled up from the dirt and glided forward along the ground, writhing like snakes gliding forward as a pack. The tips burrowed into the dirt and the tree moved forward. Closer. The leaves stilled, the tree stopped, and the bellowing resumed.

Shane tried to pull away, but Delik's grip on his arm tightened.

Kyle screamed and struggled in vain to free himself. The Scalpers were too strong, and carried him across the field toward the tree.

Each time the bellowing stopped, the leaves rustled in the tree and it moved, until it stopped in a square of tilled earth and waited.

Shane twisted against Delik's grasp and tried to run, but the Scalper held firm. Even if he had broken free, Shane would have stopped. Along the edge of the clearing he noticed other trees that shook in time with the one in the field, and even thought he heard them echo the sounds.

"Hum the note, it's the only way." Delik pulled him closer. "You can't leave. Kyle's plot is yours now."

Kyle pleaded for mercy, but the Scalpers did not stop. Even across the distance of the field, Shane heard the Scalpers humming. A softer, more subdued note came from the crowd at the edge of the road.

Branches from the tree stretched toward Kyle and grabbed him, lifted the old musician away from the Scalpers. The group of men in black overalls backed away, still humming as they went.

Shane took a deep breath and held it for a moment, trying to settle his nerves. He focused on the sounds around him: the bellowing of the tree, the hums from the Scalpers and the crowd. Even the leaves whispered the note when a breeze gusted through them.

"Hum the note," Delik said. "You're our new sing-songer."

The tree quieted and lifted Kyle skyward. Its leaves shook, a few fell off and lilted toward the ground. The note seemed to be the key to salvation, keeping the people of Hyerton safe even though it called to the tree.

Shane hummed. He matched the A note and held it for as long as he could, but his voice wavered with fear. The note faltered. He drew in a deep breath and began again, humming the A note along with the crowd.

The tree pulled Kyle down close to its trunk, beside an ear-shaped knothole, just below the lower branches. It held him there for a moment, as if listening to the sound from his throat. When Kyle stopped to breathe, the tree shook him again and pulled him taut. Each time he breathed, the tree pulled him apart a bit at a time.

Shane gasped a quick breath and continued humming. He glanced at the people of Hyerton, standing in a line along the road, humming their notes and watching Kyle. Their chorus of voices would not falter all at once. Their notes could continue on, together, though each stopped individually to breathe. Kyle could never hum alone longer than they could together.

Spindly branches twisted around the old musician, a little at a time, with each of his breaths, until Kyle's screams overcame his humming. The tree tore his arms from his shoulders, and its roots dug holes in the ground. The tree ripped Kyle to pieces, tossing his flesh across the square of tilled earth, burying the pieces in the fertile soil.

Shane watched the tree back away across the field into the woods, knowing he could never escape Hyerton. The villagers softened their humming as it went. He heard a groan in the crowd and saw the barkeep hunched over, clutching her pregnant belly. Shane stared at her, wondering how often the trees came out to the fields, Delik's words turning in his mind: "Kyle's plot is yours now."

The End

Raitt Black is a reformed dreamer who, despite the ill intentions of the universe, or perhaps because of them, consistently claws back to live among society's norms. At a young age, Raitt was abducted by the written word and devoured stories of all kinds. His favorites usually involved monsters and mythological creatures, which he purposely moved around the library in the hopes of hiding them from the librarians.

Horror

This penchant toward stealth and subterfuge naturally lead him to an appreciation of the macabre, where all is not always as it appears. It was within the gray, the shadows, and the unexplained that Raitt found love, awe, and wonder. His writing strives to share that same dichotomy with his readers.

Raitt's first book, *The Dain Princess*, is available through raittblack.com

Arachnight

Angela J. Maher

Brian sat up in bed, forcing muscles and joints to move that would rather stay immobile. Old Mr Archer, they called him. Yes, he was old, but so was everybody else in this dingy, stinking facility. Why did he get "Old" added to his name? Maybe he was the eldest, he didn't know. His breath came in short gasps as he finally got himself somewhat upright. Anyone would think he'd just climbed a dozen flights of stairs. After a long moment, he swung his legs over the edge of the bed, and lowered his bare feet to the cold floor.

The nursing staff had begged him to eat his dinner, but he'd refused. The homogenous glop they'd served up had made his stomach roil just looking at it. So what if it was designed to fill his nutritional needs, it wasn't real food and he would not eat it. He knew they suspected he was starting to show signs of dementia, but unless they put a monitor on him, or his door, to stop him wandering, he didn't care. He also knew they thought he'd be the next resident to drop off the perch. He could understand why, looking at the stick-thin limbs protruding from his pyjamas.

Brian stood up, stifling a groan. Straightening his back, he shuffled across the floor, opening the door to his room a crack. He peered with his good eye down the hallway, as far as he could. There was no movement in the gloom. He held his breath and listened. Nothing. He hadn't expected anyone to be around, but had to be careful. It was time to track down some proper sustenance. It had been a long time since he'd done this, but he felt weaker than he ever had before.

He slowly opened the door, creeping out into the hallway, before gently closing the door behind him. He checked and oiled the door regularly, to make sure it didn't squeak the way most of the doors in this wretched place did. He hadn't bothered putting his gown on, and the chilled air made him shiver. It didn't matter; what he needed wasn't far away. His steps came quicker as his eyes adjusted to the near darkness. His eyesight was one thing that had never

Horror

failed him. Well, in his good eye it hadn't, at least.

He came to the end of the hallway and paused near the door to the last room. Loud snores emanated from inside. On a bad night he could hear them from his own room. He started to reach for the doorknob, then snatched his hand back. No, not tonight. He carefully moved around the corner and into a small foyer, the doors leading to the garden in front of him. Glancing up at the security camera, he breathed a sigh of relief. The dangling cord and missing lens attested to the fact that it still hadn't been fixed, after Alfie had attacked it with his walking stick several days earlier. Poor Alfie, his paranoia had finally got the better of him. He'd been moved into the secure wing now. Brian didn't expect to see him again.

He eased the door to the garden open, turning the lock to the open position before closing it and moving off into the darkness. It was even colder out here, with the brittle grass under his feet damp, small stones jabbing him. Brian didn't care. He was out, free. Maybe not for long, but it still counted.

2

Clattering shoes and the squeaking wheels of a trolley woke Brian from a pleasant dream of a sandy beach and a submissive blonde. He opened his eyes and blinked in the watery light that was trying to illuminate his room. The sight of his room never failed to cloak him in a mist of depression. It was the best he could afford, having no family to support him, but there were very few places he'd lived that were worse. The worn linoleum floor curled up at the edges. The walls, painted a neutral shade of nothing, had shadows of mould that no amount of bleach seemed to shift. The furniture was old, mostly plastic, mostly at the end of its useful life.

He sighed, closing his eyes to block out the reality of his surroundings. He should just leave, move on and start again elsewhere, but he just couldn't get motivated enough. He was old. Older than his records said he was. He'd seen, and done, so much. He'd been happy for a while, he'd loved, had adventures. Then he'd been alone, and he'd stopped caring about just about everything.

The door burst open, and a way too cheerful voice said, "Time to wake up, Mr Archer. Let's get you up, and ready for breakfast, shall we?"

Brian opened his good eye and glared at the petite young lady who was busily gathering his moth-eaten slippers, and grimy, but comfortable, gown. What was her name? Becky? Becca? He sat up in bed before she could offer any assistance, shoving his feet into his slippers before she could see the dirty soles. He stood, and allowed her to help him into his gown, as she always did.

"You're looking better this morning," she said. "I thought you might be coming down with something when I read in your notes that you didn't eat last night."

Brian grunted. "Grabbed something later," he said. "Slept well."

"You're lucky then. Marjorie said she was kept awake all night by somebody snoring. I suspect there might be a few more sleepless residents tonight, once they hear the news."

"What news?" grumbled Brian.

"There was a murder just down the road last night," she said, her voice low. "A particularly nasty one, from what I've heard. Police thought it was an animal attack at first, but the victim's wallet had been emptied."

"Sounds gruesome. How'd you find out about it?"

"The police came to speak with our nightshift staff, to see if they'd seen or heard anything. A homeless guy that lives in that burnt out factory down on the corner said he saw an old man wandering around. Couldn't have been anyone from here though. You're all either monitored, or too smart to go gallivanting around in the cold." Becky assisted him across to the bathroom, but gave him privacy when she saw he was steady on his feet.

Brian took his time, thinking. He hadn't noticed being observed during his midnight walk, and that was disturbing. He'd always prided himself on how aware he was of his surroundings. He simply could not get caught. If he was, they'd assume his wandering was due to dementia, and start monitoring him at night. No more nocturnal jaunts would be the end of him.

Breakfast was served in a communal dining room. Becky got Brian seated at his usual spot, and brought him over a cup of coffee. The cloudy, grey liquid looked more like dishwater, and tasted worse, but the caffeine was welcome. He forced himself to eat a few pieces of toast, aware of being watched carefully. If he wanted to be left alone, he needed to be seen eating regularly. The toast was always cold and slightly chewy by the time he got his. The jam was surprisingly good though, homemade, he suspected.

He asked for a second cup of coffee, just so he could observe the other residents for a while longer. News of the murder had indeed spread, and his breakfast companions were unusually animated. Dorothy, a kind but constantly anxious lady, was crying. Bob and Ben, identical twins who were still inseparable at 82, were talking excitedly with one another. Iris, her mauve hair askew, kept repeating "Murder! Hmmph!" as she glared at everyone around her, as though she suspected one of them was at fault. The staff looked frazzled as they constantly fielded question after question. Brian felt not a shred of sympathy at the long

Horror

and frustrating day they had ahead of them.

Becky saw Brian push his chair back, and go to stand. She hurried across to assist him, her brows knitting as she discovered he didn't need her. Brian noticed her expression.

"The old joints are feeling good today. Must be the change in the weather," he said.

Becky glanced out the window, still puzzled. It was a little sunnier than it had been recently, but nothing out of season. "I guess so," she replied, taking the arm Brian now held out to her. As she accompanied him back to his room, his feet dragged slightly, but he clearly didn't need her to find his balance. She didn't comment on the further lack of help he needed to change into his day clothes.

"Do you need me to help you down to the games room, Mr Archer?" Becky asked.

"Huh? Oh. No, not today. I have a letter to write first. I'll call someone when I'm ready to head down," he replied.

Becky nodded, and left the room. Brian breathed a sigh of relief. He liked the girl, but she was so damned observant. Cute as a button, too, now that he thought of it. He shook his head, annoyed with himself. Having thoughts like that about her would only lead to trouble, or, at the very least, embarrassment. Still, if he continued to feel better…

Brian removed a box from the chest of drawers by the door, and sat on the better of his two chairs. One of its plastic legs flexed alarmingly, but thought better of hurling him to the floor. He took a key from his pocket, and unlocked the box. Inside were a number of old photographs, and a bundle of letters tied together with a faded ribbon. He lifted one of the photos out. It was of himself, many years ago. He was dressed in a soldier's uniform, his posture straight, his body strong. A neat moustache decorated his lip, almost black, just like his hair. The girls had all quite liked him back then.

Brian jumped as another staff member came barrelling in the door. He slammed the box shut, but the photograph was still in his hand.

"Who's that then?" the carer asked as she stripped his bed, peering over her shoulder.

Brian smiled a little. "Oh, just me, in my prime," he replied.

The woman, a little too plump and a little too nosy, in Brian's opinion, stopped her work to come over a take a closer look.

"Nice costume, very authentic," she said.

"Oh?"

"Yes. Even you aren't old enough to have been in the army *that* long ago.

My husband is an historian," she explained.

Brian grunted and slipped the photo back in the box when she turned away again. The woman, he had no idea what her name was, started babbling on about the history of army uniforms, and telling Brian what pieces her husband had in his private collection. Brian didn't bother correcting any of her numerous mistakes. He just knew that if he started talking to her, he'd never get rid of her. She eventually finished up, and left with a smile and a nod, oblivious to his dislike.

He waited for a moment, and then returned the box to its customary position, checking it was locked. He left his room, and slowly walked down towards the games room. His shoulders sagged as he contemplated the boring day he would spend there. Now that Alfie was gone, he had nobody to play chess with. He could join the daily group trip to the shops, but they'd wonder where he'd got his money from. They didn't need to know how much he had, or where he got it. One of the few advantages in living in a place like this, with it being understaffed, was being able to keep secrets. He'd rather keep his secrets than buy a new hat, or some other stupid thing he'd never wear or use.

3

The day had eventually drawn to a close, with Brian glad to escape into his room and close the door. He'd feigned sleep when a staff member had popped his head in to check he was safely in bed. The sounds of movement in his wing of the building had dwindled into silence, and only then did he sit up. It was still an effort, but his clandestine meal the night before had strengthened him enough that he didn't need to pause long before making his way across the room.

He hadn't intended going out again so soon, but as he'd climbed into bed, he'd had the abrupt urge to do just that. He'd let himself atrophy for far too long. Once he'd got a bit more cash together, he would pack up and leave. His one taste the night before had reignited his will to live. To really live, not just exist in a crumbling, decrepit body.

He let himself out the same way as before, and crept along through the shadows in the garden until he reached a low stone wall. Glancing back, he squeezed in behind a shrub to a clear, hidden pocket where a tree had died and had never been replaced. Shivering slightly, he stood on the rough stump and removed his clothes, his sun-starved, wrinkled skin almost luminescent in the moonlight.

Brian took a deep breath, closing his eyes. A shudder ran through his body. He stretched out his arms and arched forward in a grotesque mimicry of a tai

Horror

chi move. His skin darkened, and a crackling, tearing sound could be heard. His bony limbs thinned even further, elongating, turning black, coarse hair sprouting. His body shortened, and his stomach distended. A series of wet pops heralded more long black limbs erupting from his ribs. His body lurched, shuddered once more. The transformation was complete.

The gigantic spider, that moments before had been Brian, climbed up onto a hedge that bordered the road. The twisted, unkempt branches disguised the spider's shape as it moved smoothly, silently along. Exposed to the sky, it was safest up here. No bird of prey could ever possibly tackle it, and humans, the only real threat to it, rarely looked upwards. Unless they heard something, that was. It placed each leg smoothly and with care, lifting it up and reaching out for the next branch if the first one threatened to crack. The spider's progress was slow. It was still weak and needed to feed several more times before it would be back to its prime.

The hedge ended at a crossroads. The spider descended to the ground, the tips of its legs feeling for vibrations to alert it to anything, or anyone, approaching. It could feel the hum of busier streets nearby, but nothing close enough to be a threat, or a meal. Silently it took a left turn, hugging close to the walls of the buildings set against the footpath. Ahead, on the corner, was the burnt out factory. The spider paused and felt for vibrations once more. At first there was nothing, but then yes, there was a faint stirring from inside the shell of a building. Its next meal awaited.

The spider scaled the wall of the factory, squeezing through an empty, yawning window frame, then abseiled silently to the floor. Piles of blackened debris and rubbish obscured its view of the interior, but the vibrations were stronger now. Black limbs reaching, searching, testing, it made its way across to a pile of boards in the corner. No, not a pile, a shelter, a crude hut built by the man hidden inside.

The tip of one arachnid leg felt along the edge of the entrance to the hut. It scraped audibly, just a little bit, and the stirrings within abruptly stopped. The spider waited, and then scratched a leg lightly down the side of the hut. It felt its prey shift, startled. Fresh blood always tasted like nectar, but the addition of a little adrenaline made it all the sweeter. The spider reached around to the back of the shelter, scratching the crude wall once more.

"Who's there? What do you want?" The voice was loud, but a tremor shook his words.

The curved hook at the end of one of the spider's legs prised its way under a board at the shelter's rear. It pulled, and the board protested with a slow groan. A sharp tug and the board started to dislodge. A startled cry came from within the shelter. There was a flurry of panicked movement and the makeshift door at the front was flung open. A figure catapulted out, straight into the waiting embrace of the spider.

The spider wrapped itself around its victim, legs holding him close and tight. The man tried to scream, but the spider bit down into his soft stomach, piercing flesh with razor sharp fangs, venom silencing any attempt at a worthless cry for help. The man twitched in a dance of death, his eyes rolled back in his head, a trickle of blood leaking from the corner of his mouth. The spider drank the warm, flowing blood, not bothering to liquidize its meal, or wrap the body in silk.

Thirst slaked, the man's body was discarded, a broken pile amongst the rubble. The spider moved away, languorous, taking a long moment to clean its glistening legs before leaving the building the same way it had entered. The street was silent and still. No witnesses this time.

4

Brian was already awake and out of bed when Becky came in to assist him. He'd added a beanie to his disreputable morning ensemble, the hat pulled down low over his ears. He tried not to smile at her double-take at his odd appearance.

"Well..." she said, not quite hiding a smile of her own. "It's nice to see someone is going to make my day a little easier. Feeling cold, are we?"

"Just a little," said Brian.

Becky took his arm to guide him down the hallway and felt a shiver of disquiet. Brian had always been skeletally thin since she'd started work there, six months prior, but today his arm felt strong, filling out his sleeve instead of swimming in it. He must be wearing an extra layer underneath, she decided. Either that, or she was losing her mind.

Becky watched Brian out of the corner of her eye as he ate breakfast. There was definitely something different; it simply couldn't be her imagination. She risked taking a good, long look at his face as he turned his head to speak to one of the twins. She felt a cold sensation wash over her. The lines on his face were noticeably reduced. She'd studied his face before, fancying she could see the ghost of the handsome young man he'd once been, but now he almost actually looked young. She turned away, feeling a tremble start in her hands. When she glanced back, having helped another resident out of their chair, he was gone.

Becky was kept busy for the next hour. The morning was particularly chilly, which maybe explained Brian's ridiculous headwear, and many of the residents were finding it harder to move around as a result. Despite the workload, she

Horror

couldn't keep her mind off Brian. What was going on? She'd always been accused of having an overactive imagination, but she didn't think that was the case this time.

When she eventually managed to leave the dining area, she headed directly for Brian's room. She was scheduled to assist him with his shower, if he requested it, and required to remain nearby even if he declined her help. She knocked on his door, waited a moment, and then entered the room.

"Mr Archer? I'm here to help you with your shower."

The room was empty, but Becky heard a shuffling from within the bathroom. She strode across the room, tapping on the door before opening it without waiting for a reply. Brian hastily jammed the beanie back on his head, but not before she saw his hair. The strands were now dark brown, almost black, rather than the wispy grey cloud she'd only ever seen him with. She froze as he glared at her. Brian darted around Becky and slammed the bathroom door shut.

"You saw, didn't you?" His voice was rough, but strong, not that of an old man.

"I… I don't know what you're talking about." Becky shrank back against the wall.

"Yes, you do. I saw you watching me this morning, too. If you say anything, I will kill you," said Brian, standing over her.

Becky closed her eyes, heart pounding. She could feel the nearness of his body, from which a faint, earthy odour emanated. A shiver went through her as she felt him move even closer, physically pressing her against the wall. She jumped as the tip of an ice cold finger stroked her cheek.

"You really are very pretty," said Brian. "It would be a shame to hurt you, to spill your hot, red blood, and rob you of your last breath. Although, it's not like you lead much of a life. You're working in this dump far too many hours to have anything worthwhile going on outside of here."

Becky opened her eyes and tilted her head back. Brian's face was close, his sharp blue eyes boring into her. She felt a fresh wave of adrenaline at the close-up sight of his impossibly rejuvenated features. She was trembling, but did her best to look defiant.

"I have a life." Her voice came out broken. She cleared her throat. "Ok, so I can see something is happening to you. What could I tell anyone? That you're getting younger? Nobody would believe me. Nobody listens to me when it comes to normal stuff, so why should they? How about you tell me what's going on, and maybe I can help you."

One corner of Brian's mouth lifted in amusement. He stepped back a little, and the return of Becky's personal space felt like an open window to her.

"Help me?" he said. "Why would you? You're just trying to save your own skin. Nice to see you've got some sort of backbone though. Too many women I've known just melted into a puddle of tears."

He moved back even further, but leaned against the door, blocking her exit. Smiling a little, he removed his beanie. His hair was thick and glossy. Becky tried to tell herself it had just been dyed, or was a wig, but everything else about his appearance told her it was unlikely to be the case.

"How can this be possible?" Becky's voice was little more than a whisper.

"Perhaps I should show you," said Brian. He took in a deep breath, then, as he slowly exhaled, his mouth widened with a wet, tearing sound. His teeth blackened then shrank back into his jaw, which morphed into a wicked pair of mandibles. He sprang forward and clamped his hand over Becky's open mouth as she went to scream. As tears streamed from her eyes, his mouthparts gnashed together in front of her face, before transforming back into their former human shape.

Becky's face was white, and her legs were visibly trembling. She gasped for breath as Brian released his hand from her mouth, and she slid down the wall onto the floor. She covered her face with her hands, letting out a soft moan.

Brian looked down at her without sympathy. It had been such a long time since he'd indulged in a little bit of terrorising. Even so, he felt a grain of disappointment that she'd succumbed to tears after her earlier bravery. Such a pretty young thing, it would have been nice to have had an ally like her for a while. He watched as she took her hands away. She took a few deep breaths with her head bowed, then slowly looked up at him. She was still frightened, but now a spark of awe lit her eyes as well.

"What are you?" she said, her voice wavering.

"I am not your average elderly resident," said Brian dryly.

"I can see that. So what then? Is it voodoo? Devil worship?"

Brian laughed softly. "Devils aren't worth worshipping, and voodoo is a cover for something much more sinister. No, I can simply become youthful again by feeding on others."

Becky stared hard at him. "What, like some sort of vampire?"

"Sort of," said Brian. "But not like any vampire you've heard about. Feeding on the blood of humans makes me young again, but I do not need it to survive. Sunlight and garlic aren't an issue for me either, and I don't turn into a bat. I am a spider."

"Spider?" Becky's expression had changed to something Brian could no longer read. "Can you spin a web?"

Horror

"I can, but I usually don't. Takes too long. All I need is some blood, so no dissolving my victim's guts either, just slash and drink."

Becky looked up at Brian, head slightly to one side. "I've always had a thing for cobwebs," she said. "The way they feel, the way they look. I used to cry when my mother swept them from the corners of my bedroom."

She put her hand to the collar of her shirt, hesitated, then pushed the fabric down to reveal a tattoo. A delicate cobweb decorated her upper arm, small but intricate. "All I need is a spider."

Brian felt like he'd lost control of the situation. Of all the possible scenarios he could have imagined, this was the last one he would have. The way she was looking at him stirred something primal in him, and he moved closer once more.

"One more victim and I'll be fully restored to my prime," he said. "I'll be leaving then. If you come with me, I guarantee your life will become a lot more interesting."

His offer surprised even him, but there was something magnetic about the curve of her jaw, the depth of her blue eyes and the clean scent of her body. Becky's dreamy expression hardened into a serious mask. Her direct, unflinching stare made him feel oddly threatened for a moment, but then she smiled.

"You know, I am kind of bored with my life. Tell me when and where, and I'll be there," she said, her posture daring him to change his mind.

"The factory," he said. "Tonight, midnight. I'll know if anyone else is there, if you're thinking of setting me up."

"I'll be there," she said. "This whole things scares me, but I can't help but feel that I was meant to meet you."

5

A thin drizzle softened the angles of the dark street as Becky strode through inky shadows on her way to the factory. Her backpack strained at the seams, and pulled heavily at her shoulders. She shivered, but whether it was from the cold, or something else, she wasn't sure. Stopping at the corner, the quiet stillness of the night engulfed her.

The drizzle was strengthening into rain when she saw a figure walking along towards her. Hands in pockets, he moved unhurriedly, his wet hair shining under the streetlights. A duffle bag was slung over one shoulder. As he came closer, Becky recognised Brian. He now looked no older than 30. His handsome face showed no sign of wrinkles, and his body moved with powerful grace. Despite knowing the monster that lurked beneath, she felt an instant pull of attraction.

As Brian came alongside her, Becky fell into step with him, and they walked silently through the streets.

As they approached the train station, Brian steered her into the driveway of a small motel. He took a key from his pocket and ushered into the first unit inside the property. Becky wrinkled her nose at the musty odour, her face showing clear distaste as she looked around at the outdated interior.

"I have tickets for the first train out in the morning," said Brian. "The station is closed overnight, so I thought this was as good a place as any to wait until then."

He dumped the duffle bag on the floor, and took off a leather jacket Becky had never seen him wear before. She didn't ask where he'd got it. She was almost certain she'd seen an identical one on a guy she'd often crossed paths with when walking to work. Becky suspected he was missing more than his jacket now.

Brian stood in the middle of the room, watching Becky. The jacket had kept his upper half mostly dry, but his hair and jeans were saturated. She had been sensible enough to wear a rain jacket, but her own jeans looked wet as well.

"Guess we'd better dry off," said Brian, one eyebrow quirking up.

He sat on a cracked, ugly chair and unlaced his boots. Tugging them off, he was thankful they'd kept his feet dry. Cold didn't bother him in his youthful guise, but he hated the feel of wet socks. Looking up, he saw Becky had yet to move, even to drop her own heavy looking bag.

Standing, he locked eyes with her, before pulling his t-shirt up and over his head. It wasn't wet enough for him to need to take it off, but the look on her face was the objective he was after. She broke eye contact with him, a blush on her cheeks, and looked away. Her eyes darted back to him as he began to remove his jeans. He could feel her watching as he peeled off each leg and draped the garment over the back of a chair to dry. He moved to stand in front of her, wearing just his briefs. Becky's soft mouth was parted slightly, her eyes roving over his bare skin.

"Aren't your clothes wet too?" he asked, a teasing note in his voice.

Becky said nothing, but finally dropped her bag to the floor. She took her own shoes off, wincing as one rubbed at a new blister. The sodden socks peeled off inside out, revealing blue tinged feet, small and perfect. Her eyes refusing to meet his, she removed her jeans and placed them on a chair next to his. A knit pullover came part way down her pale thighs, hiding everything but her legs. She jumped as Brian gave a little tug to the sleeve.

"What about this?" he asked.

"Dry," she said, voice cracking slightly.

"I think you'd feel better with it off."

Horror

Brian closed the last of the distance between them, put his arms around her and gathered her to him. She pulled uselessly back from him for a moment, before allowing her body to mould to his. She could feel the contours of his body through her clothes, the strength of his muscles obvious. Slowly, avoiding eye contact, she crept her arms around his waist. She looked up as a deep groan went through Brian.

He took the opportunity to lock his mouth to hers, his kiss hard and unapologetic. She felt a thrill of excitement at the contact of his lips, his teeth, his tongue. He relaxed his grip to remove her pullover, revealing a snug t-shirt underneath. His hands moved across her body without hesitancy. Becky gave a shriek as he picked her up and dropped her roughly on the bed, but didn't resist as he removed the rest of her clothes. Naked himself, he joined her on the bed, kissing her once more. Becky broke the kiss and pushed him away from her a little.

"What's the matter?" he asked. "Not enjoying yourself?"

"I… yes… I am. But…"

"But what? You must have known this would happen," said Brian, taking her hand and kissing each fingertip, one by one.

"Could… could you do something for me?" she asked.

"Anything to get you hot," he purred in her ear.

"Could you spin some silk? Just a little? I want to feel cobwebs against my skin."

Brian looked at her eager face. "You do know that means I'll have to become a spider?"

She nodded.

"Ok sweetheart. I promise not to bite, so promise not to scream."

Becky closed her eyes as the metamorphosis began. She lay still as his arms pulled away from her, to be replaced a moment later by a cold, hard limbs. She felt a sharp claw gently caress her side, and opened her eyes to see a massive black spider crouched above her. Gasping, she watched as he began to spin silk, his legs delicately gathering it and placing it around her body. At the feel of the cobwebs on her skin, she moaned with bliss. The spider changed back into Brian, and he pulled her to him once more, wrapping the cobwebs around them like a shawl. The strands were soft like gossamer rather than sticky.

As Brian allowed his desire to take over, Becky looked up at the stained ceiling, a smile on her face. It had been so long, oh why had she abstained for so very long? Her arms gripped him as he moved above her, and she gave free rein to her own lust. A primal shout from Brian was immediately followed by a snap and a tearing noise. Becky moaned in sensual delight and flung her arms above her head.

Blood spattered across the room. Brian's head, separated from his body, rolled to the floor with a dull thud. Becky rolled his body over, straddling it as she bent her head and lapped at the blood oozing from the stump that was his neck. One hand narrowed and blackened, forming a claw. She split his chest open and took out his heart, drinking the contents like wine. What a shame it had to end this way, but for her spiderlings to have any chance at survival, she needed to drink their father's blood.

It had taken so long to find another of her kind. Something about Brian had always attracted her attention, but it wasn't until he'd started to change that she'd known. Licking her fingers clean of his blood, she was thankful he hadn't realised what she was. He had been old, experienced, but her own age, long forgotten, had given her the skills to mimic a female human to perfection.

Later, she left the motel unit door open as she moved off into the dying night. She would use one of the train tickets Brian had purchased to find a new home. A quiet town somewhere would be ideal, somewhere to grow her spiderlings until they were old enough to mimic children. Then they would move on once more. She hoped for more than one child this time.

The End

Angela J. Maher is a stay at home toddler wrangler, daydreamer, bibliophile and happy introvert. She is a member of the Tasmanian Writers Centre and is based in Hobart. She has had several pieces of flash fiction published online, and has a number of longer projects in development. She loves to read just about anything, which is reflected in her writing; anything goes in both length and genre. After graduating with a Bachelor of Science with Honours in zoology, she worked a variety of jobs, including archivist and laboratory technician.

You can find Angela on Twitter @AngelaJMaher and Facebook www.facebook.com/AngelaMaherAuthor She would love to hear from you.

Absent Friends

John Lau

The first time Connie saw the 112-year-old house that would be her new home was on the fourth day of the long drive from Ames to Eugene. Her husband Jeff had rented the two-bedroom, one-and-a-half bath, two-story on his last trip out, less than five hours after signing his new employment contract. He'd spent the rest of the day driving the tree-lined streets, familiarizing himself with his future environs. It was a process he had gotten good at, having done it before: three times in the past five years.

The house itself was indistinguishable in appearance from its neighboring, wood-framed domiciles. What made it remarkable was the rent—several hundred dollars less than the other homes he'd considered, all similarly sized and work-adjacent. It would give his young family a chance to get out of the hole, perhaps even get ahead if the job lasted. It was enough to give him hope. And although Jeff Salt was still in his early 30s, hope already seemed a commodity that had proven itself elusive.

"It's not exactly Club Med, is it?" Connie said they sat at the base of the narrow gravel drive, the Volvo's hood ticking from the heat of their trek.

Jeff looked over to gauge her disappointment and saw her suppress a smile instead.

"I did good?" he asked.

Connie unbuckled her seatbelt and reached for him. He smelled of the road and tasted like coffee, but so did she. "You did good," Connie said.

It was good for the two of them to reconnect. For too short of a time it had been just them. They'd planned to delay parenthood, but the Universe had plans of its own. Those plans were now strapped into the backseat of the Volvo C30, twisting a plastic Transformer robot into shapes the manufacturer never dreamed possible. Jeff and Connie turned to their son like a single entity divided into two halves.

"What do you think, buddy?" Jeff asked.

Alan played with his toy, making explosion sounds with his mouth.

Connie got out and opened the rear door. "C'mon, Alan. We're home now." She lifted the boy, now almost five years old, from his seat. He waved his robot through the air and made flying noises.

"Ugh. You're getting too big to carry, kiddo." Connie said. But she didn't set him down.

The house was already bustling with activity. The movers, unimpeded by the biological demands of a preschooler, had arrived hours in advance.

Across the street, a couple who looked to be in their 80s walked their slow-moving dog. Nearby, another retired resident localized fallen leaves with a lawn blower.

"How sweet. We've moved to Leisure World. I'll bet the block parties here go on for days," Connie said.

Jeff grabbed a box and headed for the house. His wife was the most sardonic woman he knew. As he stepped onto the porch, his gaze landed on a thin, white haired man standing behind the knee-high picket fence that bisected their respective front yards. The man looked as if he'd once been tall, but gravity, time and the worst that life had to offer had beaten him into submission. He wore sadness the way Jeff wore sneakers. And if Connie would let him, Jeff would sleep in his sneakers.

He set down the box. "Hey, how you doing? I'm Jeff Salt. Your new neighbor."

The old man turned away and walked into his house without a word.

Connie joined her husband. "What a sweetheart. Reminds me of your dad."

"Nice. My dad's only in his 50s."

"See what he's got to look forward to?"

Jeff laughed and shook his head. "Give the guy a break. This is an old neighborhood. He probably knew the former occupants a long time."

"That's no excuse for rudeness, Jeff."

Jeff grabbed a 15-pound dumbbell out of the box. "You're right, Connie. I'll go kick his ass." Connie rubbed his shoulder.

"Wait till after we get the cable hooked up before you start making new friends."

Jeff dropped the dumbbell back into the box. "Whatever you say, dear."

Their attention shifted to the procession of their belongings migrating into the house. Connie jiggled her son. "This is our new house, Alan."

Alan stared at the open front door... or perhaps at the light and shadows that shifted just beyond its threshold. His hand rose to make a small wave.

"Hi," he said.

Horror

"Hi, house," Connie said and carried her son inside. Jeff picked up the box to follow them.

As he did, he spied a bent silhouette, standing immobile behind the neighbor's screen door.

The family settled in. Their new routines became ingrained. Then one morning, shortly after Jeff had left for work, Connie was putting away the breakfast dishes when she heard Alan speaking to someone in the other room.

"Alan. Five. Hot Wheels," she heard him say.

This was odd because, so far no one had been in the house who wasn't named Salt.

"Alan, who's here?" Connie called out.

"This is a Corvette. I used to have a Mustang too, but dad stepped on it," she heard Alan say.

Connie dried her hands and strode into the den where Alan played on the floor with his cars. She glanced around the room.

"Who were you talking to, honey?"

"Gilbert," Alan said.

"Who's Gilbert?" Connie asked.

Alan played with his cars. "The little boy."

"What little boy?"

Alan made engine sounds. Connie looked down the hall to the bathroom, walked over, looked inside, and came back.

"Where is he?"

"He went in there," Alan said.

Connie followed her young son's gaze. He was staring at a small door.

A door that Connie knew led into the cellar.

She put her hand on the knob, turned it and pulled. The door's hinges creaked. Connie peered down the narrow flight of stairs into darkness.

"Gilbert?" she called.

She groped for the light switch. A large spider skittered, inches from her hand. Connie never saw it. What she didn't know wouldn't hurt her.

Ancient wooden stairs groaned beneath her feet. Connie arrived at the bottom but went no further.

Her eyes darted around the cluttered, musty space. It had remained untouched since the day they had moved in. The realtor who rented Jeff the old house had been in the process of emptying it of its longtime furnishings. The main rooms had been cleared, even the attic. But the Salts had needed to move in before the workmen could get to the cellar. Jeff had assured the realtor that he would do it himself.

Somehow, the onerous task kept getting kicked down the road.

"Hello..." Connie called. "Gilbert, come out please. It isn't safe in here. I'm sure there's rusty nails and you can get tetanus."

A thick layer of dust blanketed everything—covered shapes, the walls, even the ceiling. Connie stared at the closest shape. The cloth covering was so faded and grimy it was impossible to tell what color it had even been. Yet it seemed to breathe, even though the air in the cellar was still.

Connie grimaced and reached for the sheet. "Gotcha," she said and yanked.

There was nothing beneath the sheet but a small table, tilted at an angle due to a loose, wobbly leg.

Connie coughed and waved to dissipate the cloud of dust she'd stirred up. She looked around the cellar. It was quiet as a crypt.

Her patience ran thin. "Gilbert, this isn't funny!"

A loud clang made her jump and grab her heart. But it was merely the sound of the home's old water heater stirring to life.

She turned away from the boiler. As she did, a shadow flashed behind her and she heard a metallic bang. Connie whirled. A hulking form loomed in the dark of the farthest corner.

It was an old refrigerator. No, not even a refrigerator. It was older than that. It was an old icebox, left over from the days when people had to purchase and store their preservative cold.

Connie knew that doors or at least the door handles of large appliances should be removed so that children wouldn't trap themselves inside. The icebox's previous owner hadn't.

Connie took a deep breath and grabbed the handle. She pulled the door open.

There was nothing inside.

No mummified babies.

No mummified food.

Not even dust.

It was in fact the cleanest, most pristine spot in the entire room.

Connie released the handle and the door swung shut. But this time, not all the way. It sprung back open.

Connie pushed the door shut and felt it latch. But when she let go, it popped back ajar. She took a step back.

"Well fuck you anyway," she said and then a shiver ran through her.

She went back up the stairs, rubbing her arms.

Safely upstairs, Connie closed the cellar door behind her and leaned on the wall. She stared at Alan, playing with his cars on the floor.

"Brrrm. Brrrrmm. Errrkk," Alan said.

"So he's got an active imagination. So what?" Jeff said. They were lying in each other's arms beneath the blankets.

"No, it's weird, Jeff. I could've sworn there was somebody there."

"So you've got an active imagination. Now we know where he got it from," Jeff said.

Connie frowned and traced a figure eight on his chest with her finger.

"Well... imagination or no, that icebox down there is definitely a deathtrap."

"I'll take the door off its hinges tomorrow," Jeff said. "Then we'll lock up the cellar till we can get it cleaned up. Okay? Don't let it bother you."

"You're the boss," Connie said and rolled over onto her side.

"Sleep well," Jeff said.

"You sleep well," Connie said.

But for whatever reason that night, neither slept well.

The next day, Connie took Alan to kindergarten.

"This is it, kiddo. No more free lunch. It's time to get swallowed up and processed into subservience to the machine," Connie said.

Alan looked worried.

"Do I hafta."

"Unless you've got a vast fortune stashed away that you're not telling me about. Yes."

Alan sighed. "Heck."

He pulled back his shoulders, stood up straight and strode into the classroom. He never looked back.

Connie felt a lump in her throat and her eyes get misty. She turned and hurried back up the sidewalk.

Her tears flowed freely as she arrived at her front walk. She stopped dead in her tracks.

Alan sat on the front porch, waiting for her.

Connie strode up to the kid, trying to look stern for his sake, or hers. She wasn't sure which.

"Sorry, mom. ...I choked," Alan said.

They threw themselves into each other's arms.

"Dress rehearsal, sweetheart. We'll try it again tomorrow, okay?"

"'Kay," Alan said.

That night, the family watched *Ancient Aliens* on The History Channel. Connie loved *Ancient Aliens* and as a modern millennial woman, controlled the remote. Jeff didn't mind. One of the show's so-called "experts" had the strangest hair he'd ever seen on a man. He wondered if the guy wore it that way off-screen as well, but imagined it to be an affectation for the show. Still, one never knew.

Alan, sharing his father's skepticism, or perhaps merely too young to care about the compelling mysteries of mankind's origins, turned and looked up at the young woman who had emerged from the wall behind the couch. She was dressed for bed in a nightgown. Her complexion was pale, her hair flaming red.

"Hello," Alan said.

The woman gave Alan a smile. The smile seemed sad.

"Shhhh," Jeff shushed.

The woman looked at Jeff.

"Can Gilbert play with me?" Alan asked.

The woman returned her gaze to Alan and shook her head.

Connie and Jeff looked at their son and then followed his gaze.

All they saw was the wall.

"Why not?" Alan asked. "Is it past his bedtime?"

As soon as they could, they found a child psychologist.

"It's nothing to be concerned about really," said Dr. Licke. "Young children often fabricate imaginary playmates. Especially if they don't have the opportunity to develop real ones."

Jeff and Connie held hands on the couch.

"Well... my job moves me around a lot," Jeff said.

"Yeah. We don't get to cultivate a lot of friendships ourselves," Connie said. "You know. You start getting close to someone and boom, you have to pack up and leave. It's painful."

"Yeah. It's gotten so that Connie and I rely on each other more than some couples might."

"And Jeff's gone so much of the day that if I didn't have Alan, I think I'd be the one going crazy."

"You'll let me be the judge of that, won't you?" said Dr. Licke.

Jeff and Connie managed a nervous laugh.

Even though he was just across the room, they spoke freely of Alan as if he wasn't there. The boy didn't notice. He was preoccupied with the Captain America and Red Skull action figures he had found ready and available in Elliot Licke's office.

"So you don't think Alan's imagination is a dangerous thing," Jeff said.

"Drop it, Skull!" Alan commanded as the Red Skull made off with a crystal paperweight.

"Playing itself is an act of imagination and is actually very healthy," said Dr. Licke. "It gives children a chance to experiment with role models."

Across the room, Captain America hurled the Red Skull off the desk onto the carpet.

"You said Alan is enrolled in kindergarten," said Dr. Licke.

"Yeah," Jeff said. And Connie looked down to hide her guilt.

"That'll be good for him. Once he starts making friends with real children, he shouldn't have a need for imaginary playmates anymore."

His foe vanquished, Captain America did a victory dance over the recovered paperweight.

"But what if we have to move again?" Connie asked.

The Red Skull climbed back onto the desk.

They put him to bed at his usual time but couldn't sleep themselves. *Jimmy Kimmel* was on TV, but the Salts would only occasionally glance.

"Maybe we could have another kid," Jeff said. And Connie snuggled closer on the couch. It was good to reconnect.

"But we're just getting by now. You think we could afford one?"

"Well, we'd have to live simpler. No vacations. No more eating out. Not as many new clothes. Forget about a second car..."

They mulled it over. It wouldn't be easy. They had lives. They had plans.

Alan wandered out of his room, rubbing sleep from his eyes.

"Hey, what's this? It's hours past your bedtime," Jeff said.

"Can I get some water?" Alan yawned.

"Want me to get it for you?" Connie offered.

"I can do it," Alan said and trudged into the kitchen.

His parents turned their attention to the TV.

"Forget about getting a flat screen."

Alan shuffled out of the kitchen, carrying not one, but two glasses of water into his room. His parents stared after him.

"Fuck the flat screen," Connie said.

She took Alan back to kindergarten and made sure he stayed. It was hard for him and even harder for her.

Afterward, she took him to the playground in the hope he'd interact with other kids. There, Alan found a jump rope. But instead of skipping it the way other kids do, Alan tied one end of the rope to the jungle gym and swung the other end of the rope himself.

"70 boogers in a dish. How many boogers do you wish? 1, 2, 3, 4, 5, 6, 7, 8..."

The other kids there pointed at Alan and laughed, but no one joined in. Connie felt her heart breaking.

Her phone rang. She wiped her eyes and answered it.

"Mom? Hi. How are you? Aw, I miss you too. How's dad? Good. Jeffrey's fine. Alan is—in school now. No, I wasn't going to say something else. Why would I want to say something else? Everything's wonderful. What's that?" Connie drew a deep breath. "Oh yeah, he's made *lots* of new friends! I wish you could *see* them. Cute doesn't begin to describe them..."

His arms tired from waving the jump rope, Alan moved on to the teeter-totter and sat on one end. Connie bit her lip.

"The neighborhood's great. It's real quiet. Of course, that's because most of the people around here are asleep by seven. Oh yes. We're close to everything. The school is just down the block. There's a supermarket around the corner. I even found a place that makes decent Buffalo Wings. I'm not kid—"

The phone dropped from her hand.

The teeter-totter had raised Alan's end off the ground, without anyone's weight on the opposite seat.

"Woo hoo!" Alan said.

Horror

Jeff didn't recognize the light-colored van that was blocking his driveway. Connie greeted him with a kiss at the front door.

"You call the plumber?" Jeff wondered.

Connie led her husband into the den where two men in white lab coats were setting up elaborate and esoteric electronic hardware.

"What the heck is this?" Jeff demanded.

One of the lab coats extended his hand.

"Mr. Salt? I'm Miles Schoen from the Department of Paranormal Studies and Research. From the university? Your wife asked us to come over."

"Something's wrong here, Jeff," Connie said.

Jeff couldn't believe what he was hearing. "Para... normal? You mean like the Ghostbusters?"

"Well, yes and no. Not exactly," said Miles Schoen. "They were just a joke of course. And I can assure you, we are very serious."

"I didn't know they studied stuff like that around here," Jeff blurted.

"We're not a very large department. In fact, it's just the two of us." Schoen gestured toward the second man. "My associate, Dan Garver."

Garver was assembling a doorway-like object. He glanced over and nodded without breaking from work. Jeff stared at his wife.

"Not you too."

Connie looked terrified. Jeff turned back to the men in white coats. "C'mon. Really. This stuff doesn't happen. Does it?"

"Well, we'll see. I mean, sure it does," said Schoen.

"What does that mean?" Jeff asked.

"It means... not very often."

"Like how often?"

"Well... like infrequently..."

Jeff had heard enough.

"Yeah? How about never? Huh? Have you personally ever seen a ghost? That's what we're talking about here, right? Have you seen any ghosts, Schoen?"

"Well... no. But I've interviewed several people who have and—"

"Come on! This is ridiculous! You guys are witch doctors! Get the fuck out of my house!"

Connie grabbed his arm. "No, Jeff wait! I called them! I saw—"

Her husband whirled on her. "What? You saw what?"

Connie looked like she wasn't quite sure what she saw.

Then with an ominous, droning hum, the room filled with eerie green light.

"I've seen a ghost," Dan Garver said as he emerged from the glow of his now operational equipment.

"Bullshit," Jeff said.

"I was 12," Garver said. "Our house caught on fire. Dad was smoking in bed. My whole family…" He halted, haunted by the last memory of his family.

"I was asleep in my room but my dog Scout jumped on my chest and started barking. I smashed out a window and made it into the yard. I looked around but all I saw was flames. No one else got out."

"Oh my God. That's terrible! I'm so sorry!" Connie said. "Your whole family! Even your dog…"

Garver shook his head. "Scout didn't die in the fire. My mom. My dad. My kid sister Elizabeth. But not Scout."

"You saved him?" Connie asked.

"He wasn't there to save," Garver said. "Scout was older than me. By the time I was 12 he was on his last legs. He'd gone blind. And then he got dysplasia. My folks decided that old, blind and crippled was enough. They had Scout put down in December of '95. The fire happened in April the next year."

In spite of his skepticism, Jeff got goosebumps. The frustration he had brought into the room went out for a smoke.

"Okay, look. I don't doubt that you guys believe this shit, but… Aw hell." He nodded at the biggest instrument in the room. "What is this thing?"

"It's a spectroscope," said Schoen. "Not the state of the art by any means, but a functional unit nonetheless. It measures and separates the characteristic of physical phenomenon."

"Of course it does," Jeff said.

"Auras, Mr. Salt. All living things have an aura. It can be felt, photographed, and sometimes seen. If you sever a leaf from a twig, its aura will remain visible for hours, as if the leaf was still there."

Connie interrupted. "So ghosts are—"

"—Somewhat the same thing, yes. Only human."

Connie shivered.

"How does it work?" Jeff asked.

Schoen adjusted a dish. "Put simply, this antenna is sensitive to the type of aura familiar to humans—living or otherwise. These instruments process the energies and express them on this screen—" He indicated the source of the green glow. "—so that this halo effect is actually a visual manifestation of our very souls."

Horror

Jeff felt something rattle inside him, but couldn't tell from where.

"But this... this is just one big, green light. How can you tell who... I mean what..."

Schoen indicated the doorway-like object that Garver had assembled.

"Each of us will pass between the two poles that Dan's set up over there. This feeds your particular characteristic into the computer. The computer will then mask each aura, so that after we've all passed through, this glow should turn white."

"But if it doesn't..." Connie said.

"You've got yourself a haunted house," said Schoen.

An electronic crackle snapped and Jeff and Connie both jumped. They looked over to where Dan Garver had just passed between the two poles. The way his hair stood from the static made Jeff re-considered his stance on the *Ancient Aliens* "expert."

"Who's next? "Garver asked.

Connie found Alan playing checkers in his bedroom. It looked like he was losing.

"Alan? Can you c'mere a second?" Connie asked. Her eyes held on the checkerboard, but no one made any moves.

She took the boy's hand and led him into the other room.

Alan refused to pass between the poles and started flailing.

"No! No!"

Connie tried pushing, and then dragging.

"It's alright, Alan. All of us did it. It's not going to hurt."

"I don't want to!"

Jeff raised his voice. "Alan. Do what you're told!"

Alan dropped to the floor, kicking and screaming.

"Oh, for Pete's sake," Jeff said. He picked up the hysterical child, carried him toward the two poles and tried to extend him through at arm's length. Alan shrieked in terror and WHAM.

The spectroscope imploded and the whole house went black.

"Now what?" Jeff said.

He got his keys and unlocked the new padlock he had installed on the cellar door. He followed Schoen but preceded Garver downstairs as the two scientists were the ones with flashlights. The fuse box was on the side of the wall, not far from the base of the stairs. It was covered with spider webs and rust. Schoen had to use a screwdriver to pry it open.

"Unbelievable. The whole box is lunched," Jeff said.

"No problem. We've got plenty of spare fuses," said Schoen.

"Here, I'll do it," Garver said.

"I'm sending you my next electric bill," Jeff said as Garver replaced the charcoaled plugs.

"That's perfectly fine, Mr. Salt," said Schoen. "We'd like to come back with some more equipment—"

"Forget it," Jeff said.

"I can understand your reticence. But it is in the interest of science."

"I don't give liquid shit about your voodoo science."

"There could be some profit in it for you. With more proof, I could secure some grant financing. Of course we're talking under the table, but..."

"Oh yeah? How much profit?" Jeff asked.

"Oh say... five or ten thousand. Down the line, of course," said Schoen.

"Which is it, five or ten?"

"Make it fifteen. But we'd also like to run some tests on Alan."

"Tests? What for?"

"Obviously there's something very unique about your son. It's not everyone who sees, much less communicates with apparitions."

"You haven't established that he actually sees—"

"We're pretty confident that he does."

Jeff pondered their offer, as well as its implications.

"No. We're trying to build a life here. Understand? A nice, normal life. We don't need a bunch of quacks looking under our beds for things that go bump in the night. And I won't allow my son to be poked and prodded and kept under glass like some kind of rhesus monkey."

Garver threw the main switch and the cellar filled with light.

"Your denying their existence won't make these things go away," said Schoen. "You haven't the slightest idea what kind of forces you're dealing with."

"Y'know, Schoen—I haven't gotten into a fight since I was in the 5th grade," Jeff said. "But I'll bet I could take your head and fit it inside his nose."

The two paranormal investigators stared him down. They were both taller than he was. Schoen nodded.

"C'mon, Dan." He brushed Jeff with his shoulder as he passed on his way up the stairs.

Garver lingered.

"I haven't gotten into a fight since I was a kid either."

He and Jeff breathed each other's air.

"Get out of my house before I call the cops," Jeff said.

"Dan!" called Schoen from the top of the stairs.

Garver turned and went up the stairs.

Jeff glared after them. Only after they had disappeared into the den did he realize that his fists were clenched.

He cast a glance around the cellar and shivered.

They tried to pretend the whole thing never happened.

When Alan wasn't in school, Connie tried to involve him in her chores. It made things slower and more difficult for her, but it seemed to be working. She saw no further episodes.

Jeff was tired after work but still played dad when he came home, as well as on weekends. It was football season, so the boys would watch all the games on TV.

Afterward, Jeff took Alan into the backyard to teach him how to both throw and catch the oblong ball.

"C'mon, Alan. You can throw it harder than that!" Jeff said as he lofted the ball toward his son.

An instant later it sailed over Jeff's head and over the fence.

"Touchdown, Bills!" Alan yelled.

None of the Salts had so much as seen or even heard a peep from their unpleasant next-door neighbor since the day they moved in. If they were lucky, maybe he might have passed away inside his house months ago. If so, he wouldn't mind if Jeff just climbed the fence and retrieved his son's football. Still, it was a good idea to knock on the guy's door first, just in case.

Much to Jeff's dismay, the old man appeared in the side window.

"What do you want?" he demanded.

"Oh, hi. I'm Jeff Salt. This is my son, Alan. We live next door—"

"I know who you are. What do you want?"

"Our football went in your yard," Alan said.

The face disappeared from the window. Alan and Jeff exchanged a glance.

"I'll just buy you a new football," Jeff said.

Then the front door opened.

The furnishings were as old and uninviting as the inhabitant. He stood aside to let the Salts pass by.

"Thanks. We appreciate it," Jeff said.

Alan used his father as a shield from the mean-looking old man.

"Hurry up. You're letting in the flies," the old man said.

They found the football in the overgrown backyard, floating in a goldfish pond, green with algae. Jeff picked it up and dried it in the tall weeds.

The old man was looking out his front window as the Salts hurried back through the house to the front door.

"Thanks again," Jeff said. "If you need anything, just knock on our door." He didn't really mean it.

The old man just stared out the window, but Jeff wasn't expecting a response.

"That's the lady!" Alan said. And both men turned to look.

He was pointing at a framed photograph of a young woman, dressed in the fashions of the 40's. Her skin was very pale. And in a technique that had been popular back in its day, the black and white picture had been hand-colorized so that the woman's hair was flaming red.

"Alan—let's go," Jeff said.

"That's Gilbert's mommy!" Alan cried.

Jeff looked at his neighbor in embarrassment but was shocked to see that the old man was staring at them and was now ashy white.

"That's Gilbert's mommy!"

Jeff took his son's hand and dragged him out the front door. He heard it lock behind them.

After they had gone, the old man shuffled over to the dusty, framed photograph and picked it up in a trembling hand. He didn't remember when he'd looked at it last. It was a lifetime ago.

He sat by the window until the sun went down and his house filled with darkness.

The next weekend, Connie took Alan to Buffalo to celebrate her parents' 35th anniversary. She hadn't planned on going but her folks sprung for the airfare.

Horror

Jeff spent the rare opportunity to relax reading a detective novel on the couch in his underwear. When the doorbell rang, he had to hunt for a pair of clean gym shorts.

His next-door neighbor stood on the front porch.

"Hey. What's up," Jeff said.

"Mr. Salt? My name's Gilbert White. Is your son home?"

"He's at his grandparents' for the weekend. Why?"

White looked crestfallen. Jeff let the door swing open.

"You want to come in?" He didn't really mean it.

Jeff had little experience interacting with people so much older and wasn't quite sure how to behave. He offered the man a drink to be polite, was surprised when White accepted and had to search for something that contained alcohol. He uncovered a pint of Jack Daniels that had somehow survived his bachelor party. The two of them sat on the couch and made small talk. It was awkward at first but became more personal with each refill and the men found common ground. Hopes and dreams, fulfilled and dashed are universal and cross generations.

After awhile Jeff remembered that White had something on his mind and realized that if he just stopped talking about himself, the old man would get to it. They sat for a few minutes in inebriated silence.

Then White stared into a distance that only he could see and told him the story.

"Clay Beamish and I were neighbors since the time we were boys in short pants. Clay right here in this house, me next door like I am now. We got in Dutch together, took our licks together, and dammit when the time came if we didn't go and fall for the same girl. Of course there were some prettier than Anne Warden—but none of 'em quite did it for us the way she did. No sir. She had a way about her that made you feel like every day was Saturday morning. And every night was New Year's Eve. Clay and I... we had a little bet as to which of us would get to marry that skinny redhead."

White contemplated his glass. "I was Best Man at their wedding."

"Mazel tov," Jeff said. He held out his glass and the two men toasted.

"Well... I chased a few other girls after that, but none like I did Anne. Never really cared when they'd slip away neither. Nope. Sport that he was, Clay named their baby after me too. That was part of the bet, see. Thank God it was a boy. I get gas whenever I think there could be a woman running around named Gilberta..."

Jeff smiled but the old man wasn't kidding.

"At any rate, along about this time, Tojo decided to redecorate Pearl Harbor. And so like everybody else, Clay and I went down to the enlistment office to join up... That was the first time I ever heard the word 'hemophiliac.'...I'll never forget the look on Clay's face when he realized he was leaving me behind with Anne."

White was no longer in the room, or even the 21st Century. He was remembering what it was like to be 19 years old.

"To our credit, we held out long as we could. Almost a year. But I guess she and I both came to realize it was... unavoidable."

The silence lasted so long that Jeff wondered if that was the end of the story.

"Those were the happiest three years of my life. War and all."

Jeff refilled his glass.

"Naturally, we tried to stop when Clay came back... but we just couldn't. None of us was very happy. We all just tried to pretend it wasn't really happening. Finally Anne told me she was taking the boy and leaving Clay. And the next day... she was gone. Clay and I stopped talking after that. 69 years without even a 'good morning.' I... couldn't bring myself to go to his funeral last spring. And I never heard from Anne again."

The years passed in a blur behind the old man's gaze. He was now sitting on a couch, seven decades later, in the house of his former best friend and romantic rival. In the house of the only woman he had ever truly loved. In the house of an innocent boy who might even have been his own son.

A tear that had been held captive for so long it was almost dry escaped down a crevice in the old man's cheek.

He looked Jeff in the eye.

"You know where she is, don't you."

Jeff felt himself getting ill.

It wasn't from the booze.

Connie steered the Volvo into the driveway and honked the horn. When Jeff didn't come out of the house, she honked it again.

She got Alan and their suitcase out of the car.

"Jeff?" Connie called as they entered the house. She set down the suitcase. "Jeff?" She went out to the backyard.

Alan ran into his room, grabbed his Millennium Falcon and flew it back out the door. Only later would he notice the note tacked to his bulletin board, scrawled in Crayola:

GOODBYE ALAN. GILBERT

Horror

He passed his mother in the hall on his way to deep space and she flattened against the wall to let him pass. That's when she heard the muffled scraping and pounding that seemed to vibrate through the house.

She followed the sounds to their source. When she got to the cellar door she heard her husband's voice cry out.

"Oh my God!"

She heard a loud moan that sounded like a large animal dying.

"No! Wait! Don't!" she heard Jeff cry.

There was a thunderous explosion.

"Jeffrey!" Connie screamed and threw open the cellar door.

Jeff whirled at the sound of his wife's voice. He was covered with dirt and sweat. He looked like he'd seen something he would never unsee.

"Connie—don't come in here!" he cried.

But she was already at the foot of the stairs. And Connie too would never unsee the hole torn through the brick wall of the cellar with hammers and picks.

She would never unsee Gilbert White sprawled like a broken toy, the .45 caliber pistol by his hand, the grey matter that had long held his memories now a cloud of red mist.

Nor would she ever unsee what was on the other side of the wall.

A skeleton her size. And another the other the size of her son.

It was too late to do any good.

But Connie still screamed.

They pulled Alan from school and Connie took him to Buffalo for a while. Kindergarten is about socialization and could be restarted. He was still very young.

The job in Portland had been promising, but Jeff found one that paid almost as much and offered similar opportunity in Spokane. After signing his employment contract, he drove the tree-lined, work-adjacent environs and found a house he thought they could afford.

It was summer now and Connie could hang their laundry on a line in their new backyard. A friendly-looking woman, about a decade older leaned on the low fence that separated their yards.

"Welcome to the neighborhood," Connie's new neighbor said.

"Thanks," Connie said. The lines the smile made on her face were deeper now and permanently etched. As were a few other ones.

"Don'tcha have a dryer? C'mon over and use mine," the new neighbor said.

"We've got one, thanks. It's just such a hot day, thought I'd take advantage. Besides, it heats up the house."

"Yeah. I just turn up the air conditioning full blast."

"We're trying to keep our utilities down. Hi. I'm Connie Salt." She went to the fence to shake hands.

"Marie August," the new neighbor said. "You like loud, drunken, all-night parties?"

Connie looked at her in surprise. The woman didn't seem the type.

"Haven't been to many lately. Why?"

"I got three teenagers. You don't have much of a choice."

The women shared a hearty laugh.

"What about you?"

"Just one. He's gonna be six."

A look of deep concern crossed Marie August's face.

"Oh really?"

"Yeah. What's wrong?" Connie asked in alarm.

"Well, I guess the realtor sure wouldn't have toldja."

Marie lowered her voice. "A few years ago there were a lot of little kids disappearing in this neighborhood. It was awful! The FBI even came in. But they never caught the guy. Then it just stopped. I'm surprised you hadn't heard. It was all over the news."

"We're from out of state," Connie said. She felt a hole grow in the pit of her stomach.

"Just don't leave him alone," Marie said. "If you ever need a babysitter, I'm right next door. And the girls can help out too."

Connie smiled in appreciation. But she was already having second thoughts about Spokane.

She was folding the laundry on the bed when she heard Alan talking in the living room.

"I'll be your neighbor," she heard him say.

Connie left the laundry unfolded and ran for the living room.

"Alan!" she cried.

Alan turned around and said "What?"

He was alone in the room, watching *Mr. Roger's Neighborhood* on TV. The show, no longer in first-run episodes was still timeless and would educate children for generations to come.

Horror

Connie fixed herself a drink before finishing the laundry.

"We're going to the zoo today, boys and girls," Mr. Rogers said on the Salt family TV. They still had their bulky, tube television, but it still had a good picture. The flat screen could wait.

"And we're going to see all the animals. They have lots of different kinds of animals there. Can you name some of them?"

Alan loved Mr. Rogers and wished *he* had been their neighbor in Portland.

"Well, they have lions and monkeys and giraffes and elephants. Can you say elephant, boys and girls?"

But Alan had friends here in Spokane. Sixteen of them in fact. All of whom he'd met one by one on the first day after he'd moved into his new house.

They sat with him there on the floor.

"Elephant," the children said.

The End

John Lau is a Los Angeles based screen and TV writer. His first novel *Phantom Pain* is available on Amazon. Despite its title, it's not a ghost story.

Nasty Little Nightmare

V. Jáuregui

For CB

She didn't understand the offer at first, but nobody does; not really.

She moved with the agility of a flying insect, the wooden floors didn't register her lithe step. A long trail of wickedness, a history of lies, there was no other way to describe her. And there she stood, an innocent looking figure surrounded by children; pretending to care while gloating over the secret knowledge that it had been her who threw the cockroaches into the pot of soup. The familiar rush of adrenaline hit her pleasantly when she heard the first disgusted scream—a horrified thirteen-year-old girl who discovered a not quite dead insect at the bottom of her plate. It was a silly trick, completely beneath her, but she had to fill her day. Feeling thrilled, her senses enhanced; she ran to the large dinner table and oozed words of comfort. Boys and girls looked at their plates with sick fascination. They wondered how they had not seen the cockroaches. Had they eaten one already…alive, perhaps? She told them not to worry, knowing very well that her overacted revulsion was all they needed to see.

People were drawn to her, particularly children. How ironic that those she hated the most felt so at ease in her presence.

After a long journey, she retired to her quarters. It was a night like many before. She locked the door to her small bedroom and was about to take her clothes off when a strange smell attacked her nose. It was putrid. Her brain offered two possibilities: a dead mouse? A plate with old food? On her way to open a window she sensed a change in the atmosphere, a light twist in the order of things.

Horror

There was a loud ringing in her ears. She was conscious and her eyes were open but it was not the austere furnishings in her bedroom that she saw. A colorful mosaic of images and sounds floated before her—secret moments from her past, dark deeds. Blood trickling down her mother's chin. Coveted objects. Chubby arms of babies she had hurt. Dirty water in a forgotten bathtub. Bodies with eyes in all the wrong places.

The orgy of images shifted through the room, enveloping her delicately. It then condensed into a cloud-like substance, formed a circle and disappeared.

Her body felt both alive and spent. She did not question the experience. Why would she? Every second of it had been ecstasy. Dragging her feet, she approached the bed, too tired to look up at the clock. How long did she stand there, hypnotized? It was not important. She noticed a strange piece of creamy paper on top of the pillow. Her heart started beating faster and she momentarily lost focus. The smell, that foul smell was back. She took the paper with uneasy fingers, fondled it, wanting to read it and the same time not! In the end, she gave in. Bold letters, hand-written in black ink relayed a plain offer: "JOIN US"

She read it a hundred times, and as she pondered, demons giggled with delight.

She walked the halls quietly the next morning. Things she saw every day looked different. A casual observer would think she was a happy woman going about her day and he would have been right—happiness has different meanings to different people. It is a fact that some are born twisted, it is also a fact that while most people resist evil, there are those who embrace it.

Even if her brain didn't understand the note's origin, the rest of her body did. The sense of familiarity was strong, as if she had seen it before. She had always felt oddly misplaced, unsynchronized to others, but today she knew better things were in store. The threat of a real smile landed on her mouth; she was on her way to the music room, her unfashionable shoes clunking loudly, when she heard high-pitched, wailing sounds. She stopped cold and tried to tune her ears to the source. Like a human antenna she turned and walked and walked and turned until she found it: kittens! A box full of kittens in a storage closet, and what a glory they were!

In the face of danger, any animal will die to protect its young, but there was a sense of resignation in mama cat's attempts to defend her litter. It knew what it was up against but still hissed and growled helplessly as it was held in place by a heavy foot against its tummy. It scratched and drew blood at an enemy that took each kitten and pressed it between both hands until minuscule bones cracked and it stopped breathing. It was early. Her day had only started.

She was always discrete—delivering tiny drops of poison whenever the opportunity presented itself. It was not her style to throw an obvious blow. Young girls in need of a guiding word came to her with their problems. She offered sensible solutions, provided practical and prudent recommendations; then waited patiently with a loaded stinger, like an anxious wasp. She had learned that the right amount of information at the precise moment could create chaos when it was uttered in a perfectly innocent voice. Tiny drops of poison.

She had corrupted many, and did not intend to stop.

The day was long, the anticipation unbearable; she could not wait for it to be over to go back to her bedroom. Something or someone would be waiting for her. She didn't much care who that someone might be, the only thing that mattered was that she saw, she SAW. She had been allowed to see and re-live every single moment of pain she had ever caused, to savor the knowing eyes of a no-longer-innocent child. How many people have the opportunity to experience their most enjoyable moments more than once? Her mind was made up. She would join them, whoever they were; she felt part of them already.

She heard the music as soon as she entered the bedroom. She closed the door and in a moment of clumsiness, slipped and fell to the floor. Her head felt heavy, like a balloon filled with water. "Join us,"—the voices chanted—"Be us." The music was louder, small objects flew lazily over her bed, and yet nobody came to the door, nobody wondered if everything was all right. Why did this realization bother her?

She crawled, trying to stand up, wanting to understand why her body felt like it belonged to someone else, but the voices didn't allow her any thoughts. "Dance! Dance! Dance!"—they ordered—and for the first time in her life true fear set in.

Her will was strong and she did not give in easily. On hands and knees, hair covering most of her face, she lifted her head in an unnatural way. Something was inside her, something old and spiteful. The muscles in her neck tensed painfully as she howled in the darkness.

"Dance, dance, dance!!" Her body didn't quite hold her but she did her best to comply, and as she danced, sweaty impish hands held her. She danced until she couldn't move, and the knowledge came to her in broken pieces. Once again, she was allowed to see the cloud, a massive tissue of evils past that enveloped her with the urgency of an unwanted caress. Oblivious of the yellow eyes that watched her, she accepted her faith: she had been bested.

A chair moved on its own and she heard muffled laughter as she tried to keep her balance. Standing on a chair, she learned, was not an easy task after hours

Horror

of dancing.

Her body and spirit would be transformed into fuel. Her malignant essence was a precious commodity for those who feed on evil. Standing high on the chair, her mind became a mind in transition. Nothing mattered anymore; she became a dark footnote, a nasty little nightmare. Unseen forces pushed the chair from beneath her feet and oxygen slowly left her lungs. The quality of the thick fabric around her neck was the last pleasurable sensation she ever registered.

CORONER RELEASES CAUSE OF DEATH FOR "GIFTED" NUN, SCHOOLTEACHER

(NY Press) After much speculation, Catholic church authorities were forced to make a public statement regarding the death of a loved music teacher and counselor found dead in her quarters.

The deceased nun, a thirty nine year old music teacher and counselor, was found with a scarf around her neck; the scarf was tied to an old ceiling pipe. Last week, the New York City medical examiner's office ruled the death as a suicide by hanging.

The headmaster at St. Bernadine's Middle School said he was not aware of any issues and stated that the school community was "devastated, shocked and deeply saddened by the tragic news" he added that according to feedback from school personnel and fellow nuns, there had been "no apparent signs of distress."

The End

Veronica Jáuregui started reading science fiction and horror at a very young age, her grandmother; an avid reader of horror, pulp magazines and comics, encouraged her to write. As a child, she loved frightening her classmates with her stories and hopes to do the same to her readers. Her stories, "A Filthy Habit," "13 Days After the Storm" and "The Lake" were published in the *Writers' Anarchy* series.

Veronica's inspiration is nothing more than daily life, she tries to find horror in the mundane, and does her best to show the dark side of what we perceive as familiar. She is inspired by the classics but is always looking for new books to read.

Veronica was born in Los Angeles, CA and lives in Rosarito, Mexico. You can reach her at authorveronicaj@gmail.com.

Made in United States
Orlando, FL
30 November 2023

39564926R00095